Mistaken Marshal

A Novella

Also by Crystal L Barnes

Acclaim for Crystal L Barnes

"Ah, the old west... cattle drives... fathers who insist on choosing their daughters' husbands even from the distance of the grave. We're treated to all those elements in Crystal Barnes' debut story. One of the appealing aspects of this entertaining western is the author's use of humor. Who doesn't love a good laugh at the expense of a hunky cowboy?"

—VIRGINIA SMITH, AUTHOR OF *A HOME IN THE WEST*, REGARDING *SIGNED, SEALED, & DELIGHTED*

"*Love, Stock, and Barrel* is one of my new favorites. This fun story has it all: a spunky heroine, an evil father set on ruining her life, and a Texas setting, which always makes me smile. I particularly loved the romantic thread in this story because it was laced with a bit of intrigue, which kept me flipping pages to see how (or if) things would work out. The writing is lovely and the storyline has something for everyone. Highly recommended!"

—JANICE THOMPSON, AUTHOR OF *MISMATCHED IN TEXAS*

"As a Pastor and an avid Western fan, I often have to overlook things in the books I read. This time I didn't need to overlook anything. This is a well-written, exciting Western Romance with plenty of action, adventure, and romance. The fact that it is written from a Christian perspective for me was all the better. Unlike some 'Christian' fiction books that come across as either preachy or with the Christianity tacked on as an afterthought; *Win, Love, or Draw* was just a western romance that happened between to characters that could have been real life Christians. They struggled and feel short at times but they kept striving to live as Christians. The action was fast, the adventures were thrilling, and the romance was at times sweet and at times rocky and at times passionate. I loved this book and really loved the plot device of marriage as a waltz the author used."

—REV. GEORGE H MCVEY SR,
AUTHOR OF THE REDEMPTION TALES SERIES

"When a Crystal L Barnes book comes into my house, it goes to the top of my to-be-read pile. I know it will be a delight to read, whether it's a full-length novel or a novella like *Husband Hunting*. The novella is a delightful read with plenty of humor, a cowboy, and a feisty heroine. With plenty of plot twists and turns, it kept me turning pages until I finished reading the last page."

—LENA NELSON DOOLEY, ECPA, CBA, AND PUBLISHER'S
WEEKLY BEST-SELLING AUTHOR OF *RESCUING CHRISTMAS*,
AUTUMN LOVE, AND *A HEART'S GIFT*

Mistaken Marshal

A Novella

CRYSTAL L. BARNES

To God be the glory.

*Lo, I am with you alway, even unto the end
of the world. Amen.*
Matthew 28:20

*Trust in the L*ORD *with all thine heart; and lean not unto thine
own understanding. In all thy ways acknowledge him, and
he shall direct thy paths.*
Proverbs 3:5–6

Prologue

O nce upon a time in a land far, far away—"

"No, no, no." Eleven-year-old Andy sat up on his pallet in the middle of the cabin's living room floor. "Not one of those stories, Grampa. One of *your* stories. From the old days. You know, with the outlaws and shootin' and showdowns."

"No." Dalton popped up from his place beside his big brother and added his two cents. "I want to hear a story like Robin Hood."

"A love story, Grampa." Six-year-old Madelyn, the youngest, squeezed her doll tighter and cuddled closer into her grandmother's side on the couch.

Beau Bones sat back in his rocker. "A love story, shootouts, and Robin Hood, huh?" He scratched his jaw.

"Gramma, can you think of a story like that?"

"There is one that comes to mind." She shared a conspiratorial grin with him as she stroked their granddaughter's dark curls from her brow.

"You think they're ready for it?"

"Yeah!" Andy said.

"Please, please, please, please," Dalton begged.

Leaning forward in his rocking chair, Beau pitched his voice to a mysterious tone. "The year was 1875."

The boys snuggled back down in their blankets, the firelight from the hearth dancing across their eager faces.

Beau leaned back in his chair and let the years drift away. "The days were hot, and the Wild West was still alive and well in Small Tree, Texas."

Chapter 1

Small Tree, Texas
August 1875

Living the life of Robin Hood wasn't what it was cracked up to be. In fact, Jodie Ross was getting mighty sick of it. Especially when dodging bullets. She knew she should've stayed with the horses like usual.

"Jerry, I oughta skin you alive for pickin' this town. I told ya we had enough, but would you listen to me? No. Now look at us." Another round whizzed by her head, making her duck back beneath the windowsill. She flicked a short strand of dark hair out of her face to glare at him. "We're like fish in a barrel in here."

Her much older brother continued to fire out the broken window of the general store with nary a glance her direction or hint of worry to his tone. "Did ya leave the horses where I told ya?"

"Of course. But I don't see how we're gonna get to 'em with half the county shootin' at us."

Jerry gave Dix and Pat a nod before tugging down his gray bandanna and exposing her to that wild grin she'd learned to fear. "You know I always got a plan, Jo."

A plan? What kinda plan would get them outta such a tight spot? The last time they'd been holed up like this, it'd taken—

"No. Oh no. Jerry, you wouldn't. You didn't. You promised."

"Aw, don't be such a stick-in-the-mud, Jo. Live a little." Grinning all the while, Jerry grabbed a barrel of pinto beans and shoved it up next to her other side.

Dix and Pat darted back into the room and crouched their large frames behind the oak counter. A heartbeat later an explosion shook the building and shattered what little glass remained on the windows and shelves.

She was gonna kill him. That's all there was left to it. Because if she didn't, they were all gonna end up dead. With ears ringing and gunpowder stinging her bandanna-covered nose, Jodie socked her brother in the chest, scrambled to her feet, and stepped over the unconscious form of the storekeeper. She darted after the others, leaving Jerry to grab up the remaining loot and supplies.

The short distance between the now gaping back end of the general store and the oak grove behind the small town felt like a country mile as Jodie dashed across the grassy expanse. By the time she entered the trees, flying lead splintered the bark above her head.

She glanced over her shoulder for Jerry.

"Don't stop. Keep goin'." He tossed the bag of foodstuffs into her arms and grabbed her elbow, propelling her forward until they reached the horses she'd staked near a small creek.

Dix and Pat already galloped upstream, heading toward the rendezvous point.

More bullets slammed into trees as she snatched Blossom's reins from a nearby branch. Their pursuers were getting closer.

"Hurry up." Jerry circled his horse in the water.

"Go. I'm right behind you." For once he listened. Loud splashing accompanied Jodie's hurried clamber into the saddle. Dropping the bag's handle around the saddle horn, she sank spur.

Something black and tan bolted through the trees right in front of her. Blossom reared with a squeal. Before Jodie could react, she found herself tumbling heels over head.

Another horse bolted from the trees to Beau's right, making the wild galloping cease and his crazed horse rear, sending him tumbling backward to the ground. He hit the dirt hard, seconds before something slammed into his air-deprived chest. At first he thought it was the beast, until the assault continued. An elbow connected with his stomach. Another with his jaw.

Blinking away stars and gasping for breath, Beau did the first thing that came to mind, a move that'd occasionally worked on his brothers—he pinned the smaller person's arms down with a bear hug.

"Let me go!"

"Easy. I'm not—"

A boot heel connected with his shin. "Jerry!"

With a grunt, Beau tightened his hold and seriously considered granting the kid's request when a shout from his right stopped both their movements.

"Hold it right there." A short man broke through the trees, a shotgun in his hands, both barrels aimed at them.

Another lanky fellow stumbled into the creek-side clearing and halted, straightening. His dishwater brows rose. "He caught one of them?"

"One of who?" Beau glanced at the dark-haired kid in his hold, a kid who wore a bandanna covering all but his wide blue eyes. A bandanna? What on earth had that spawn-of-Satan horse gotten him into?

"See if you can find the others," Shorty ordered.

The troublemaker turned his head, causing the bandanna to slip, revealing smooth cheeks without a hint of stubble.

"Right." With a nod, Lanky hurried toward the water.

Without warning, the kid sank his teeth into Beau's arm and broke from his hold.

"Ouch! Why, you little brat!" Beau snagged the boy's leg, knocking him to the ground, and pinned him in the wet sand. "I ought to turn you over my knee."

"We're going to do worse than that."

At the new voice, fear flickered in the kid's eyes.

Keeping his hands on the young man's shoulders, Beau looked up to find a well-dressed, if winded, older gentleman standing next to Shorty, gun drawn.

"Nice work, mister. You just caught yourself an outlaw."

An outlaw? Beau glanced down at the youngster whose voice hadn't even changed. He couldn't be more than thirteen or fourteen. How could someone so young already be an outlaw? Troublemaker, yes, but outlaw?

"Where are the other three?" the gentleman questioned.

Shorty cocked his head toward the water. "Lawson went

to see if he could find their trail."

"Mr. Grimes, perhaps you should lend Mr. Lawson a hand."

With a nod, Shorty took off as another man approached, horses in tow.

"Mr. Hewitt, toss this fella a rope and help them, please, sir." The dapper gentleman took the horses' reins from the balding man Beau had met at the livery earlier that day and turned to Beau. "I believe Mr...."

"Bones," Beau offered as he accepted the rope from Hewitt and set to binding the outlaw's hands.

"I believe Mr. Bones and I can manage this one on our own." The leader paused, drawing Beau's gaze upward. The bearded man looked from Beau to Satan's Spawn—or Buster as the horse was more commonly known, a name which now made much more sense considering his aching backside—and back again. "Bones? Are you any kin to our late marshal?"

Beau finished securing the knot, one perfected by what his brothers used to use on him through the years, and hauled the youngster to his feet. "Yes, sir. He was my uncle."

"Well, looks like you two were cut from the same cloth."

Beau wished that were true. His namesake had been brave, fierce, afraid of nothing and no one. He was the only one who'd ever believed Beau could amount to something, could do more than struggle in his brothers' shadows. He'd hoped by coming to Small Tree, Texas, he could prove his uncle right. Prove everyone else wrong. Prove that he could be his own man. But on his first day in town, he couldn't even ride his uncle's horse.

"I'm Mayor Arthur Jones." After shaking Beau's hand,

the graying gentleman led the way through the trees, the prisoner between them. "I assume you're here to settle your uncle's estate, Mr. Bones. Are you going to be in town long?"

"Well, I, uh…I'd thought to stay on awhile, but—"

"Wonderful. We could sure use a man like you around Small Tree. As you can see, trouble has already found us in the short time since your uncle's passing. My condolences, by the way."

"Thank you."

"What would it take to talk you into staying on and being our new town marshal?"

Beau couldn't help laughing at the outlandish thought. "Not much, bu—"

"Stupendous! You're hired."

"Hired? Wait. What?"

"The job comes with a monthly stipend, plus room and board." The mayor kept talking, but Beau's brain couldn't take in any more.

Hired? Him? A marshal? He didn't know anything about being a lawman, only the wild tales his uncle used to spin when he'd come to visit. Tales a little boy with seven older brothers could only imagine experiencing. He couldn't fill his uncle's boots, not in a thousand years, not in ten thousand. The mayor was highly mistaken if he thought Beau could handle such an important job. Sure, he'd always dreamed of such a chance, but he couldn't…

He wouldn't…

It wasn't right to let the mayor, the town, think him capable—

The outlaw stumbled, breaking Beau's inner argument and his grip on the kid's arm. The boy pivoted toward the trees.

"Oh no, you don't." Beau had tried that move with his brothers too many times to count. Snagging the youngster's waist, he tossed him over his shoulder.

The mayor angled him a grin. "See, I knew you were the right man for the job the minute I laid eyes on you. This way, Marshal. I'll show you where you can lock up this prisoner. Then we'll send for the judge."

At the praise, Beau couldn't help standing a little straighter. Maybe he *could* do this job. Maybe this was the exact opportunity he'd prayed for almost all his life. Maybe, just maybe, if he tried real hard, he could prove the mayor hadn't just made the biggest mistake of his life by making Beau Bones the newest marshal of Small Tree, Texas.

Jodie couldn't get off the new marshal's shoulder soon enough, but she could've lived forever without hearing the resounding clank of a latching cell door. The harsh smack of metal upon metal echoed all the way to her core, chilling her to the bone even in the August heat. A simple bunk, a single window, and a host of iron bars surrounded her. How had her life come to this?

"You might as well sit down, sonny." The one called Mayor Jones handed the large key ring to the younger rat with the dark brown eyes, broad shoulders, and way-too-fast reflexes. "You're not going anywhere anytime soon."

"That's what you think," she mumbled.

"What was that?"

Stiffening her spine, she faced the dandy. "Nothin'."

Her brother wouldn't leave her there to rot. He'd get her

out.

Marshal Bones settled a hand on the bars, his handsome face coming much too close to a look of compassion. "What's your name, kid?"

"None of your business. And don't call me kid." The man had a lot of nerve calling her a kid. He only had a few years on her at most. Probably couldn't be but twenty-three, surely not old enough to call her "kid."

"You wouldn't want to tell us where the others went, would you?"

Jodie crossed her arms and glared in response.

"That's what I thought." The dark-haired lawman turned to the mayor and shrugged. "It didn't hurt to ask."

"Keep working on him. Maybe you'll find out something." The mayor donned his bowler hat over his pristine silver and brass locks. "I'll let you know as soon as the search party returns, and I'll get that telegram off to the judge for you. You go on and settle in here, and I'll let you know what I find out."

"Much obliged, sir."

"I'll also have Mrs. Lottie send two plates over from the boardinghouse." Mayor Jones stepped to a door just past the left end of the cell and opened it. "Your uncle stayed in here when he had prisoners to watch. Sometimes even when he didn't if the boardinghouse was full."

"Thank you, sir. This'll be just fine." The lawman paused. "If you don't mind, can you ask them to bring my things over from the boardinghouse when they come with the food?"

"Of course. That shouldn't be a problem. Mrs. Lottie's boys are dependable lads."

"Good to hear." Bones fiddled with the keys as the mayor

headed toward the exit. "By the way, what did this kid do?"

"He and his gang robbed Haskins General Store before they blew up the backside of it."

The strapping lawman swiveled her direction, eyes wide. "You *what*?"

Offering him a smirk, Jodie strode to the bunk and plopped onto the gray blanket covering the lumpy mattress. She was gonna wring her brother's neck for getting her into this mess. Her gaze strayed to the mesh of bars…

If she ever made it out of here.

Beau stared at the baby-faced whippersnapper sitting on the bed inside the cell. How could someone so young get into so much trouble? Sure, boys got into trouble at all ages, but blowing up a building? He had to see that for himself.

"Mayor Jones." Beau rushed to the door and caught the man stepping off the boardwalk. "Mayor Jones, sir."

The gentleman turned around. "Was there something else?"

"Yes, sir. I, uh… Could you point me in the direction of the general store? I just arrived in town today, and I figure I should see for myself—"

"If there are any clues. Great thinking. You'll probably want to talk to Mr. Haskins too. I'll introduce you. Follow me."

Clues? Haskins? Was that the store owner? The mayor knew more about being a marshal than Beau did. He'd better learn fast or everyone would know what a fraud they'd hired. Lengthening his stride, he hurried after Mayor Jones.

Chapter 2

If that marshal menace didn't step outta the office soon, Jodie was gonna explode. Pacing across the tiny cell once more, she tried to ignore the sounds of trickling tea splashing into a tin cup and the unwelcome urges it evoked.

She wasn't sure how much longer she could maintain her dignity and abstain from using the chipped chamber pot under the bed. She should've taken care of such business while Bones was out doing whatever he'd been doing, but she hadn't needed to go then and she'd had no idea how long he'd be gone.

"Kid, you're driving me crazy with all that pacing. Can I get you a book or something?"

Jodie sprang on the offer. "Yes, please." Anything to have a moment of privacy.

With a nod, Bones set his cup on the desk. "I got just the thing right here." He stepped to the bag two boys had brought over with supper.

Muffling a groan, Jodie sank onto the mattress, her heel bouncing with the urgency coursing through her.

The marshal crossed the short space between them and extended a black leather-bound book through the bars.

"Don't you have a book in your room or something?" Wrinkles scrunched his forehead. "You don't want this book?" Jodie sprang from the mattress and snatched it away from him. A Bible? Of all things. "If I read this, will you *please* lock the front door and go to the other room for a minute?"

"Do I look that stupid?" He folded his arms. "I never did search you. Do you have some kind of something to pick the lock on you?"

She did have the fork from supper in her boot, but she wasn't about to tell him that. Besides, she had much bigger concerns than picking locks at the moment.

"You do, don't you?"

Her attention darted to those too-keen eyes of his. If she didn't get better at hiding things, he was gonna discover all her secrets.

Bones extended his hand. "Come on, kid, hand it over."

"*If* I do have something, and *if* I do hand it over, will you do as I asked?"

"*If* you do have something, and *if* you do hand it over… I'll…think about it."

"Aw, come on. I'm not gonna do nothin'." She shifted her weight from boot to boot. This was taking too long.

"Then why do you want me to leave the room?"

"Because."

"Because why?"

"Because I want some privacy."

"Privacy? What for?"

"That's it! I can't take it anymore. My name is Jodie, not Jo like that possum-playin' storekeep said. I'm a woman, not a man, not a *kid*, and I *need* some privacy, 'cause I ain't about to use a chamber pot with you in here!"

Bones's eyes grew larger and larger until she feared they'd pop out of his head and land at her feet. His gaze darted the length of her, lingering in places she'd learned to disguise years ago when Jerry's gang members had started taking more than a passing interest in her shape.

"Y–y–you're a sh–she? H–he's a she? Y–you're a woman? I—" He pointed to his shoulder then to her then back again.

"Yeah, you hauled a woman in here like a sack of meal. Now would ya lock the door and get outta here?"

Tripping over his feet in his haste, the marshal scrambled to the front door, tossed the lock into place, and then darted to the side room, his face beet red and his eyes looking anywhere but at her.

His door barely clicked shut before she rushed to do her business.

He was guarding a woman. He was *guarding* a woman. He was guarding a *woman*! Beau struggled to make his lungs function as he gripped his knees. What on earth was he going to do? He straightened, setting his topsy-turvy world to spinning more. Gripping his hair, he closed his eyes and gulped for air and clarity.

He couldn't guard a woman, could he? Could a woman even stand trial? Why would a woman help rob a general store? Moreover, why was she dressed like a man? How old was she? How could he have hauled her over his shoulder and not known...not felt...?

Opening his eyes, he scrubbed his hands together, trying to rid himself of the burning stain. He couldn't believe he'd treated a woman with so much disrespect. He'd never done such a dishonorable thing in all his born days. Then again, he'd hardly spoken to any woman who wasn't family, and still not much even then. It never turned out well.

How on earth was he going to guard a woman, let alone get more information out of her? His hands grew clammy just thinking about it. Beau stared at the door, knowing he couldn't leave her alone too long. The town had hired him to be their marshal. They were depending on him to make sure they got justice. He couldn't quit and let them down so soon. Not to mention how that'd dishonor his late uncle's memory.

But guarding a woman? What was he going to tell the mayor? Should he tell the mayor? Was this something that would get him fired before he even started the job? Would they want to hire a woman to take his place and guard the prisoner? His brothers would have a heyday with that one.

And what about her gang? Mr. Haskins was depending on him to find out more, to get the stolen money back. If he got fired, he couldn't do that. No, he'd just have to—how had Uncle Beau put it?—bite the bullet and face the situation like a man. Yes, he'd just pretend to be his uncle. Uncle Beau wouldn't care what gender the prisoner was. He'd only care about bringing the wrongdoers to justice, about doing what was right no matter the cost.

Beau straightened. He could do the same. He could guard a woman. He could learn to be the best—or at least second best—marshal the town of Small Tree had ever seen. Screwing his courage to the sticking place, he threw open the door and marched from the room.

A squeal sent him covering his eyes and scampering behind the desk.

Jodie faced the wall and yanked her last suspender over her shoulder. "Don'tcha know how to warn a body?"

A loud crash jerked her back around in time to see the strapping marshal bouncing on one leg. Gripping his shin, he stumbled into the hat rack beside the desk and tumbled to the floor. The hat tree tumbled with him, smacking the desk then him as a host of papers slipped from the edge and buried him alive.

The pile of pages shifted and groaned, then Bones emerged, covering his eye.

Jodie rushed to the bars. "Are you okay?"

"Swell." Leaning against the side of the desk, he tipped his head back, accidentally bumping his cup of tea and sending the tan brew pouring over his dark locks. The liquid trickled down his cheeks, across his fingers, and dripped off his chin onto the mess surrounding him. "Just swell."

Placing her hand over her mouth, Jodie fought the urge to laugh until his exasperated gaze met hers. Then she lost the battle. Loud guffaws shook her shoulders, and she doubled over with uncontainable laughter. If she hadn't already used the necessary, she would've been in big trouble. Before long, deep chuckles accompanied hers, adding to her mirth.

She wasn't sure how long they laughed, but when their merriment finally faded, they both sat on the floor, staring at one another.

Jodie smiled. She couldn't remember the last time she'd had such a good laugh. That it should come the same day she got thrown behind bars, with the man who'd done the throwing no less, was ironic to say the least.

"You really oughta get a doctor to look at that." She pointed at his face. "You look like ya got the makin's of quite the shiner." Jodie had to admit that even covered in tea and with the growing color around his eye, the new marshal was a mighty handsome man.

Bones offered her a slanted grin that did funny things to her insides. "It's not the first time. Probably won't be the last."

"Really?"

"I've got seven older brothers."

"Aw…" With a nod, she turned her attention to her knitted fingers, a wave of sadness washing over her, removing the humor.

"What about you? You got family?"

Even though she knew she shouldn't, she found herself answering anyway. "One."

"Brother?"

She nodded. "But he's a lot older than me." Silence met her admission, then…

"Jerry?"

Her gaze jerked to his. "How'd you know?"

"You yelled for someone by that name before you kicked me in the shin."

"Sorry about that."

17

"It's all right. I understand."

"You do?"

"Seven older brothers, remember?"

"Right." She examined the dirt caked under her finger-nails, something she'd never allowed to stay long until she'd gone to live with Jerry in one abandoned cabin after another. Her mama had been a stickler for clean hands. Why she thought of Mama now after all these years Jodie didn't know, but something about this man made her think of the past, made her remember better times when she wasn't constantly looking over her shoulder or wondering if she'd be sleeping under the stars or a roof that night.

Sure, it was nice having something to share with the mis-fortunate folks she ran into, but honestly, she couldn't remem-ber the last time Jerry or one of the others had shared more than a glare with someone down in the dumps. They sure didn't go out of their way to help anyone but themselves.

She might as well face the truth—the only one in the Ross gang who cared about ministering to hurting people was her-self. How long had she been fooling herself? How long had she allowed herself to believe Jerry's lie, believe the men were in this for the good they could do? The answer—too long. *Her* motives might've been pure, but she was actually little more than a thief, worthy of the hate and scorn the men of this town had shown her.

Jodie dropped her face into her hands. Why had she ever listened to Jerry when she knew deep down what they were doing was wrong, that Mama and Papa wouldn't have ap-proved?

Loud footsteps and voices carried from the boardwalk outside, and the doorknob rattled. "It's locked. Marshal

Bones, are you in there?"

Bones scrambled to his feet, and Jodie did the same. She hurried to the bed as he rushed to let the mayor, the general store owner, and the other men from the search party in. That they came in empty-handed brought her a momentary rush of relief—her brother and the gang had gotten away—but on its heels worry, doubt, and the nagging question arose: Would they come back for her, or would she hang for their crimes?

"Sorry about that. Just an added precaution." Beau shut the door behind the handful of men, praying they wouldn't figure out how much of a fool he'd made of himself moments ago and praising God they hadn't been there to witness the event.

"I see." The mayor looked at him oddly.

"Can't have the prisoner getting away, sir." He swiped a hand through his hair, hoping they'd think the wetness was from pomade instead of sweet tea, and discreetly wiped it on his pants.

"No indeed." Mayor Jones glanced around the room. "What happened here?"

"I, uh…" Beau stooped and started scooping up the scattered papers. "I'm, uh, working to get things organized, but I can finish this later." He placed the haphazard pile on the desk then scooted it away from the edge when it started to teeter. "Do y'all have news?"

"Yes…I… That boy must have hit you harder than I realized earlier. Do we need to send the doctor over to look at that?"

Beau touched the tender spot under his left eye and stifled a wince. "Uh, no, sir. I'll be fine. Most every man's nursed a shiner at some point in his life. Right, fellas?" He looked to the others, who grinned their agreement. "So, the news?"

"Yes, I thought you'd like to know I finally got a response to my telegram." The mayor shook off his distraction and focused on Beau, not his eye or the messy room. "Judge Johnson will be here at the end of the month to try the case. That's three and a half weeks. I'd hoped it would be sooner."

"I say we save us all some trouble and hang him now," Mr. Haskins growled, his wiry arms folded over his wide middle, his frown no smaller than it'd been earlier that afternoon when they'd inspected the damage to his store.

The mayor's gaze strayed to Jodie, and for some crazy reason, Beau found himself holding his breath.

Haskins stalked to the bars and gripped the metal. "Where are the others, you thieving skunk?"

Jodie pretended not to hear a word, which only made the proprietor madder.

Beau kept a close eye on him even as he asked, "I take it y'all didn't have any luck finding their trail?"

"As far as we can tell, they went into the water and rode upstream." Hewitt, the livery man, scratched his bearded jaw that held more hair than his head. "We thought we found a couple of places where they came out, but the trail went dry both times. We were hoping the kid might've said something that would help us."

"Not yet."

"However, I'm sure Bones will get to the bottom of things." The mayor clapped Beau on the back. "He is, after all, our late marshal's nephew."

Beau offered a smile that felt weak even to himself. These people were going to see him for the fraud he was before the day was out, he just knew it. He had to get them out of there and fast. "I appreciate y'all coming by to let me know what you found. Maybe we can try again tomorrow."

"No sense in that." The lanky Mr. Lawson shook the hat in his hand, sending water droplets onto the scarred floorboards. "Rain started coming down on us on our way in."

As if on cue, a rumble of thunder echoed above them, and large drops barraged the roof.

Beau felt guilty at the rush of relief that washed over him, knowing they wouldn't witness his nearly nonexistent tracking skills anytime soon.

Short Mr. Grimes joined Haskins at the cell door. "Whether we like it or not, this kid's our only lead on where to find the others."

Which meant finding justice for this small town all came down to Beau's ability to talk to women. They were doomed.

Chapter 3

If this young buck was Small Tree's idea of a lawman, they were doomed to be struck by outlaws time and again. Jodie stood on the bunk inside her cell and stared out the barred window, trying to catch a breeze and getting more than a little entertainment as Marshal Bones wasted yet more bullets on a line of tin cans that hadn't budged since he'd placed them on the muddy ground twenty minutes ago.

The way he loaded, fired, and unloaded the Colt Peacemaker left no doubt in her mind that this guy didn't know the first thing about guns—which made him about the most dangerous man in Texas. If her brother tried a jailbreak, the marshal might aim at Jerry and hit her instead.

"You want me to show ya how to do that?"

Bones jumped at her voice, pulling the trigger, and finally

sent a tin can flying. He stood still as a statue, then with agonizing slowness, he turned and faced her. "Y–you want *me* to let *you* shoot a gun?"

"It's either that or risk bein' shot myself by one of your wild bullets."

"I'm not *that* bad."

Jodie cocked an eyebrow.

"O–okay, maybe I am that bad." Studying the gun in his hands, the marshal shifted his weight between his large boots, which, now that she looked at them, didn't have a single scuff mark. Mud, yes. Scuffs, no.

This stalwart man might be dressed like a cowboy with his leather vest, navy shirt, and Levi breeches, but he was a dude if she ever saw one. "What city do you hail from?"

His wide, chocolate gaze swung to hers. He opened his mouth as if to speak, then shut it and looked away. "San Antonio."

Well, at least he was from Texas. "Never shot a gun before, have ya?"

He opened his mouth, paused, scanned the meadow, then ducked his head and shook it. Straightening, he met her gaze with a lift of his chin. "I'll figure it out though."

"Hmm…maybe, but anybody can shoot a gun. It takes skill to actually hit what you're aimin' at, and with your new job, I'd say that's one skill you can't afford not to have." Jodie rested her chin in her hand. "So what's the verdict?" With a wince at her misguided word choice, she lowered her hand. "You want me to teach you while we wait for the judge to arrive? I ain't got nothin' else better to do."

Except count the days and hours and minutes. Nineteen days.

Perchance they were her last on this earth. She'd rather they be spent doing something good.

In the past four days, she'd already read most of the four Gospels. At first, she'd read out of sheer boredom, but slowly she'd come to crave the time turning pages. It'd been years since she'd laid eyes on a Bible, and she'd found the hope offered there more comforting than she'd expected, especially the passage about the thief on the cross.

That the Son of God could forgive such a worthless, guilty man as that guy had brought tears to her eyes and a prayer to her lips for the first time in many years. At the peace that had flooded her soul in that moment, she had no doubt that God had forgiven her, just like that undeserving man, but she had no guarantee He'd get her out of this situation of her own making alive. After all, sin had its consequences—the thief had still died on the cross next to Jesus—and she deserved every bit of judgment the courts decided to deal out.

"I can't just give you a gun." Bones shielded his eyes from the glaring sun overhead. "I'll be fired before I can spend my first pay."

"I can teach you a few things without ever touchin' that Peacemaker."

"Yeah? Like what?"

A hard knock rattled the jailhouse door behind her. "I'll tell ya after we eat. Sounds like lunch just arrived."

"What do you mean, 'I don't have to do this outside'?" Beau was beginning to question the wisdom of taking advice from an outlaw and not just because she was a woman. Whoever heard of target practicing inside a building?

"Empty the gun."

"What? How am I supposed to know whether I hit the target?"

"Do ya want me to teach ya or not?"

Pursing his lips, Beau emptied the revolver, the bullets pinging onto the desk. "Okay, now what?"

"You got a dime or a quarter?"

"Uh…"

"Don't look at me like I ain't playin' with a full deck. Do ya or don'tcha?"

With a shake of his head, Beau leaned back in the desk chair and dug in his pants pocket. He sure hoped no one walked in during this nonsense. It seemed like this woman had a knack for making him look like an idiot, which really wasn't much different from other females he'd met. Sometimes he wondered if he'd be better at talking to and understanding women if he'd had seven sisters instead of seven brothers, or if he was just doomed to be inept around them regardless.

The dime clicked onto the desktop. "Okay, now what?"

"You see that rear sight notch?"

The what? Beau resisted the urge to swipe a hand across his face.

"The rear sight notch—that divot on the top there."

Knowing he looked like the novice he was, Beau pointed to the groove in the metal near the back of the gun.

"Yeah, that. Balance the dime in that notch. Rest your arms on the desk…*but not* the butt of the gun."

Beau lifted the revolver a fraction. Heaven help him. Maybe he should just quit while he was ahead.

"Good." Jodie drew her pointing finger back inside the

cell and propped her elbow on the bar. "Now, line up the dime and the front sight—that metal stickin' up there on the end—with some spot on the wall there. Steady your aim, and squeeze the trigger without makin' the dime fall off."

"Okay…" That sounded easy enough. Holding his breath, Beau lined everything up and—the dime fell off.

"*Squeeze* the trigger. Don't jerk it. Try again."

Beau did. Again.

And again. And *again*.

After the umpteenth try, he dropped the gun on the desk beside the contrary dime and raked both hands through his hair. "This is impossible."

"No, it isn't. Hand it here, and I'll show ya."

He might as well.

Jodie accepted the Colt, set the dime in place, and aimed at the wall, and he was that amazed when, after five rapid-fire squeezes, the dime didn't budge. It was probably too scared to move in her presence. At the moment, he felt a little frozen in place himself.

Who could do such things?

"See. It is possible. Now here, you try."

He only accepted the revolver because she dropped it in his hands and he didn't want his uncle's prized possession to hit the floor. There was no way he'd ever be as good as her. Why should he even try?

"Go on. Take another whack at it. It took a lot of practice for me to be able to do that. You'll get it."

He didn't know about that. Besides, he doubted time was on his side. There had to be a jailbreak in the works. If he had a sister like Jodie, he wouldn't leave her behind.

Which meant Beau had better learn how to shoot—and

fast, if he wanted to keep his job.

Lifting the Peacemaker to eye level, he lined up his shot and squeezed the trigger.

Jodie watched Bones squeeze off another round, the dime remaining pretty-as-you-please on top of the gun. "Good job. You're pickin' this up faster than I expected. I think it's time we take this outside."

The dime fell off. "Ou–outside?"

"Yeah, you know that place with grass and sunshine and fresh air?"

"I know what you meant." He scratched his chin, moving closer to the cell. "I still can't let you out of there, Jodie, and they've started building in the field behind the jail."

She'd noticed. Her first guess would be a schoolhouse or a church. The building could be used for both. "You're the marshal. I'd say you can do whatever ya want."

Bones stopped walking, stopped scratching, stopped everything, and stared at her like she'd spouted some heresy. Brother, for a man with authority, he sure didn't act like one.

"You *can* take me outta here, ya know. Your job is to guard the prisoner, right? Who says ya have to guard me in here? I promise I'll be on my best behavior, and then we can practice where no one else will see."

Practice where no one else could see. Through the barred window, Beau glimpsed the meadow that any man, woman, or child could view if they rounded one of the buildings on his side of Main Street. He'd love to practice where no one might notice and realize what an amateur they'd hired. Might figure out he was taking lessons from an outlaw. But to actually let Jodie out of her cell—that was out of the question.

Wasn't it?

For well over a week, he'd watched Jodie scour the Bible like a starving man. They'd hardly spoken, save firearm instruction, which was fine with him, but he'd heard every sniffle from her corner of the room, spied every tear that'd trickled down her smooth, sun-bronzed cheeks. The words had touched her, may have even caused a change of heart.

If someone showed an ounce of faith in her, would she be willing to reveal her gang's location now? Isn't that what Uncle Beau had done for him, believed in him when no one else had? Why else would he have mentioned only Beau in his will?

Should he give Jodie a chance? The town was expecting him to learn more about her gang. Not to mention, he definitely could use more lessons if he planned to do this job with any measure of success, and he *really* wanted to succeed this time.

For once, he wanted to be able to hold his head high when he walked down the street, to have a job he felt good about, was actually good at, and could keep all on his own. He wanted to have his folks, his own family, proud of him for a change and stop seeing him as the baby who couldn't do anything without their help or who was a failure because he didn't excel in the family business. He wanted to stand on his own two feet, feel comfortable in his own skin for a change. This job was his ticket to a better life, and he wasn't about to waste that now if he had anything to say about it.

Nevertheless, letting Jodie teach him and digging for secrets meant more talking, more close interaction with a female with high, defined cheekbones, eyes the color of a summer sky, and dark locks with a touch of curl. His tongue turned to sandpaper in his mouth. How had he ever thought her a man?

And just like that, he knew how he'd get her out of town without anyone knowing he was allowing a prisoner to teach him. Holstering his inherited gun, he started for the door.

Chapter 4

In the flickering candlelight, Jodie stared first at the garment dangling from her fingertips, then at the cherry-faced lawman on the other side of the bars. "You want me to wear *this*?"

The calico dress dripped with ribbons and lace. She hadn't worn something so…so… feminine in a decade. For reasons she couldn't define, tears stung her eyes.

"I–it's too big, isn't it? I'm sorry. I had to guess at your size, and Haskins was asking so many questions. I had to tell him my sweetheart was riding into town and I wanted to have a present for her."

"You have a sweetheart?"

With wide eyes, the marshal shook his head. "I—I don't…. That is, I'm not… You see, w–women don't really find me attractive."

"Really? I find that hard to believe." Realizing what she'd admitted, Jodie gulped and gathered the gift into a ball. "I'll, uh, be sure to be dressed and ready when ya come out in the mornin'."

'Cause she undoubtedly wouldn't sleep a wink that night. The marshal was gonna let her out of the cell tomorrow. He was gonna let her teach him *outside*. He trusted her, and he'd bought her a lovely dress. She draped the flowered material across the front of her and swallowed an uncharacteristic squeal.

She was getting out of the cell tomorrow!

Beau stepped out of the side room and glanced in the cell—then glanced again.

A stunningly beautiful woman sat on the stained cot, leaning against the brick wall, her head lulled to the side, with dark, long lashes fanned across her smooth cheeks. Soft morning light shone through the barred window, accentuating her delicate face and bringing a touch of red to her dark locks. If he hadn't recognized the blue dress with the yellow flowers as the one he'd purchased the day before, he'd say a stranger had waltzed in during the night and replaced his prisoner with a curvaceous female that would take any man's breath away, including his.

Jodie looked…amazing.

Nobody in their right mind would dream of associating her with the dirty-faced kid he'd locked up earlier that month. He could hardly make the connection himself, and he'd instigated the change.

The woman was a miracle worker to make anyone think

her a man for a fleeting second. How on earth was he going to spend a day with her and learn a single, blessed thing? And asking questions—that was totally out of the question. His tongue was already tied in so many knots his stomach had given up on the competition.

Footfalls sounded on the boardwalk outside, jerking Beau out of his trance. Breakfast. Someone would bring in breakfast soon. Why hadn't he thought of that before? He had to get Jodie out of that cell before everyone knew that the *he* was a definite *she*.

Beau hurried to the desk, yanked the keys out of a drawer, and ran to the cell door. "Jodie. Jodie, wake up."

She didn't move a muscle as the barred door clanked open, and he rushed to her side.

"Jodie, we've got to get you out of here." He touched her shoulder to shake her awake.

A bony knee drilled under his ribs. His back slammed against the ground. A wiry arm pressed against his throat. Air struggled to get through.

What on earth had he done?

Chapter 5

Jodie blinked away the haze of sleep and focused on the idiot foolish enough to touch her. A handsome man with dark hair and wide brown eyes gasped in her hold.

"Bones?" She scrambled to her feet, hauling him up with her. "I–I'm so sorry. I thought you were one of my brother's gang. I—I—I didn't mean to. I'm sorry. Are you okay?"

He took a step away, holding the keys like a dagger between them.

What had she done? How could she have treated him like that? He wouldn't dream of taking her out of the cell now. She'd ruined everything with her unladylike reflexes. Sudden tears stung her eyes, and for once, she didn't stop them. She was a horrible human being.

Melting onto the side of the bed, she buried her face in

her hands. *Oh God, I'm so sorry. Why do I have to be this way? Please change me. I don't want to hurt anyone anymore.*

"Do you always wake up like that?"

Jodie jerked at the nearness of the deep voice, sure that the lawman would've gotten as far from her as possible, but he stood in the same spot, rubbing his neck.

"My brother normally kicks my boot to wake me."

"I can see why." After a final rub, he lowered his hand, his gaze steady and much too keen on her. "Other men... they've..." Bones motioned at her, a pity filling his eyes she couldn't stand.

Folding her arms, she lifted her chin. "Gotten too friendly? Maybe so, but they ain't never tried it twice."

The last one who'd been dumb enough Jerry had beaten to a bloody pulp, and that was *after* she'd deterred him with her Peacemaker pressed into his middle.

"I can understand why. I'm...sorry you had to go through that. Just for the tally books, I wasn't..."

"I know."

"In my book, women should be treated with respect. I'll, uh, remember the tip about the boot for next time."

"Next time?" Her gaze collided with his. "Ya mean... you're still gonna let me teach ya?"

"I can't blame a woman for defending herself against a perceived threat, now can I?"

He could, but the fact that he wouldn't made her want to jump off the bed and kiss him. "I promise ya won't regret it."

"Then we'd better get you out of this cell before they deliver breakfast. We need to make this bed look like someone is still in it."

Jodie hurried to help him tuck her discarded clothes and

pillow under the blanket in a convincing manner. She'd just rearranged the "legs" when a knock, which actually sounded more like a kick, rattled the door.

"Marshal, you awake?" A young voice carried through the wood.

"Hurry." Bones grabbed her hand, hauled her from the cell, and shut it behind them.

"Marshal?" Another kick-knock.

Motioning her to a chair in front of the desk, the lawman headed for the door. Their normal morning delivery boy, one of the boardinghouse owner's sons, stood on the other side.

"Why, if it isn't my new friend Arnie? I see your ma nominated you to help with deliveries today."

The freckled-face lad cocked his head. "How'd you know it was me and not Wallie? Everyone else in town gets us confused."

Jodie wasn't sure either. The boys were mirror images of each other. Although now that she thought about it, this Arnie did seem to have more freckles on his cheeks than the boy who'd brought breakfast the day before.

Bones tousled the lad's flame-colored locks. "What kind of lawman would I be if I couldn't tell two brothers apart?"

Arnie thought about it a moment then nodded. "Yeah, I guess that's truc."

Carrying the towel-covered tray, the roughly ten-year-old boy took two steps into the room and stopped dead-still at the sight of her. "Woo-ee, Mr. Marshal. I heard your gal was coming into town, but nobody mentioned how purdy she is. She sure is a good-looker."

"Yes, well, I, uh…" Bones tugged at his collar.

Jodie felt heat climb into her own cheeks, but she couldn't

hold back the smile at the lad's compliment. It'd been so long since she'd worn a dress, and the marshal hadn't said a word about her appearance. Thank the Lord for the honesty of a child. "Why, thank you, kind sir. You're a pretty good-looker yourself. Where'd you get that red hair from?"

"Thank you, ma'am. My ma says her daddy had red hair, so I guess from him." Arnie set the tray on the desk in front of her. "Sorry I didn't bring you no breakfast. I didn't know you'd be here." He glanced toward the jail cell. "My pa always used to say, 'You snooze you lose,' so I guess you can have his."

"That'd teach him not to be such a slug-a-bed, wouldn't it?"

A toothy grin parted the boy's cheeks. "Yes, ma'am."

"Then I reckon I'll take your pa's advice. Just this once."

Arnie angled his attention to Bones. "I like her." He turned back. "You gonna be here long, ma'am?"

Jodie peered toward the marshal, whose look was as uncertain as she felt. "I'm, uh, I'm not sure, Arnie. For a little while at least." Where she resided after that would be up to the judge.

Beau felt every eye in town on them as he drove Jodie past the stores on Main Street. He kept waiting for someone to rush out and demand he take the prisoner back to jail, but every man who looked their way doffed his hat with a wide, goofy grin and called out a cheery greeting. Greetings that, for some strange reason, a part of him wanted to shove back down their throats.

Only once the wagon cleared town did he feel safe enough

to breathe a normal breath. That is, until he peeked Jodie's way, and that breath lodged in his throat like a chicken bone.

Head tilted back, face angled toward the sun, the much-too-attractive woman sucked in a lungful of air, drawing his gaze to curves that hadn't been apparent the day before.

Forcing his focus toward the heavens, he tried to dispel the image from his mind and the obstruction from his throat. God help him.

"Mmm. Doesn't the air smell wonderful out here?" Jodie stretched out her arms.

He slammed his eyes shut. *She's my prisoner. She's my prisoner. She's my prisoner.*

"I really appreciate you doin' this, Marshal. I know ya didn't have to."

"Yes, well…" He tried again to dislodge the airy chicken bone. "I appreciate your willingness to teach me. We'll, uh… That is, why don't you call me Beau?"

Her beaming smile shoved the bone firmly back into place.

She's my prisoner. She's my prisoner. Clearing his throat again, he fixed his gaze on the twitching ears of the horses. "By the way, what's… *ahem*… what's your last name?"

That was a good lawman-type question, one he couldn't believe he hadn't asked in the past week and a half. Although he highly doubted she'd have answered then, and he still wasn't sure she'd answer now.

She turned toward him. "Ross. You sure are coughin' a lot. Do ya need some water?"

Ross, huh. Maybe he'd been right about the outing loosening her tongue. Ross…Ross…? Had there been a Wanted poster with that name on it? Whatever answer that might have entered his head went sky-high as Miss Jodie Ross turned and leaned over the back of the seat, offering him a view of, well, her seat.

Heaven help him.

Maybe he should turn the wagon around. There was no way he'd be able to learn how to shoot that day. If he fired a gun in his current state, there's no telling what he'd hit.

"Ah, here it is." Jodie turned and plopped back down beside him, no guile whatsoever in her gaze, and uncorked the water canteen before offering it to him with another of her distracting smiles.

The woman really had no idea of her effect on him. Turning up the container, Beau chugged the contents. Maybe he could drown himself back to sensibility.

When he came up for air, Jodie offered him the cork. "Better?"

He wasn't sure whether to nod or shake his head, so he settled with a simple "Thank you."

"So, how far're we goin'?"

"Not far." He couldn't take a whole day of this torture.

Jerry couldn't take a whole day of this torture. Tossing aside the twig he'd been skinning with his pocketknife, he headed toward the horses.

A twig snapped behind him.

With a sharp pivot, he cleared leather and aimed toward the sound.

"It's me." Pat's voice preceded him moments before his chestnut broke through the thick brush lining the cave entrance.

Jerry lowered the gun. "Where's Dix?"

"Mount up 'n' I'll show you."

Moving toward his gelding, Jerry voiced the question that'd been eating at him for days as they'd waited for sufficient time to pass before scoping out the situation. If that posse'd hurt one hair on his sister's head, he'd kill them all. Pat and Dix had no doubt picked up on his anger. Probably why they'd insisted he guard the stash while they rode to town. They'd said it was because no one would recognize them, but they probably feared he'd do something rash and get them all caught. He did too. That's why he'd gone along with their plan.

"How's Jo?"

"Asleep on a bunk in the jail."

"Did you talk to her?" Jerry made quick work of slapping leather on his mount and making sure the rags tied around his horse's hooves to help disguise the tracks were still snug.

"She's asleep. What do you think?"

Good point. That girl could sleep through a train derailing in a hurricane. Until something touched her, then look out, brother. He swung into the saddle and followed the stocky man from the cave. He'd feel a lot better if he could talk to Jo, let her know everything was gonna be all right, that he'd get her out of there. But the men were right—they had to play this smart. At least they were willing to help spring Jo. Probably 'cause they preferred her cooking to their own tasteless grub.

After traveling a few miles, Pat pulled to a stop and made a twittering whistle. A faint responding call came from a cluster of live oaks and scrub brush farther ahead. With a nod, Pat swung down.

Jerry did the same. Scanning the area, he spied Dix's mustang a distance to his left, munching on the waist-high grasses around a mesquite tree. "What're we doing out here?"

"We followed the marshal and his girl." Pat spoke barely above a whisper.

"You mean Jo's alone in town?" Jerry hissed. "Why didn't you just get the key and sneak her out?"

"The livery man was watching the place like a hawk from across the street. Besides, we need to know what we're up against."

Fighting down the urge to punch something or someone—not to mention, hating to admit that the man was right—Jerry followed Pat into the trees that lined some kind of wash. At any other time, it would've likely been dry, but after the recent rains, the creek bed held an inch or so of running water.

Because Dix was so disguised by his brown hair, vest, and broadcloth breeches, they nearly stumbled onto him kneeling between two boulders before they saw him. Without a word, he handed the spyglass to Jerry and pointed through the scrub brush hiding them from view.

A fetching brunette in a bluebonnet-colored dress stood next to a Stetson-wearing man loading a Peacemaker. More than one bullet hit the ground during the process. A star glinted on his chest as he squatted to retrieve them. Jerry followed the man's aim to a line of tin cans. Successive shots splintered the silence but not a single can.

Jerry grinned. This greenhorn was what they were up against? Snatching Jo out of his hold would be easier than a Sunday stroll through the meadow. All they had to do was pick the right time.

Chapter 6

"All right, let's see if we can do better than last time." Under the wide expanse of a shady oak, Jodie moved a safe distance away from Bones, set her attention on the tin cans, and folded her arms.

Their first lesson outdoors hadn't gone well. Not only had the marshal bumbled through setting up the tin cans, knocking them over twice before getting them all standing erect, but then he'd fumbled through loading the chambers and dropped half the bullets on the ground more than once. The man then had proceeded to try her patience with an aim she could outdo with a blindfold, a broken trigger finger, and a half dozen lawmen breathing down her neck. Hopefully, whatever had disturbed him last time wouldn't bother him today.

A shot cracked the silence. Not a single can teetered.

Swallowing an exasperated sigh, Jodie inspected his stance as another round missed its intended target. What happened to the guy who could keep a dime in place? "Are you sick or somethin'?"

Beau lowered the Colt revolver. "No, why?"

"You're shakin' like a leaf in a hurricane."

"I–I can't help it. You're making me nervous."

"Nervous? Me? How? I didn't make ya nervous at the jail, did I?" A memory of a tumbling marshal covered in tea flashed through her mind. Maybe she did.

"Can't you turn around or something?" His gaze skittered over her for the dozenth time that day before flicking back to the targets.

Well, I'll be... Why, if she didn't know any better, she'd think he found her... Naw...couldn't be. Someone like him couldn't find someone like her...attractive. Could he? For some reason a smile tickled her lips. It sure would be nice to have someone so kind, so handsome, so understanding feel that way about her, but who was she kidding? Men with his charm, connections, and character never fell for gals of her ilk. He'd be an idiot to fall for a girl who might swing before the month was out. The smile slipped away.

Pushing the wishful thoughts aside, she waved his attention back toward the line of tin cans. "Come on. You can't ask the next outlaw who crosses your path to turn around, now can ya? Only a coward shoots a man in the back, and you're no coward. Use that excess energy to hone your focus. Block out the distractions. Breathe, aim, and fire."

"Like it's that easy."

"Give me the gun, and I'll show you it is."

"Fine."

Block out the distractions, she says. Breathe, aim, and fire, she says. It's that easy. Ha! That woman had no idea what a distraction was. Oh, but she was about to.

Beau waited for Jodie to finish reloading the revolver and adjust her hands on the grips. He then stepped up close behind her as she lifted her arms and whispered in her ear, "Don't miss."

The shot went wild.

Unable to squelch his grin, he did manage to swallow the chuckle building in his throat, but all humor died the instant she swiveled toward him, inadvertently brushing his chest with her shoulder. They both froze, mere inches apart.

With a hard swallow, he forced his fingers to stay by his side, even as the air between them became charged with some kind of intensity, like the anticipation felt while a burning fuse ate its way toward a powder keg.

Her lips parted a fraction, drawing his gaze.

What would it be like to kiss her, someone with such vim and vigor? Would what he felt in that moment explode into something altogether wonderful or wound them both irrevocably?

Before he could decide, he found himself leaning toward her…until her soft gasp yanked him to his senses. He took a mighty step back, avoiding her gaze and the revulsion he'd no doubt see there. Why, he was no better than the men in her brother's gang. It'd serve him right if she turned that Peacemaker on him.

"I, uh… Excuse me." Although there really was no excuse for him or his shameful behavior. Heading toward the targets, he gave her ample opportunity to repay his forwardness with whatever punishment she wanted to mete out.

For the first time in her life, Jodie wanted to run after a man and do something more than pound him. Okay, maybe she wanted to pound Beau a smidgen, but only because she'd really wanted him to kiss her and he hadn't gone through with the desire plastered across his features. No man had ever shown her such respect, which made her want to chase after him all the more and lay her lips against his, a feeling so foreign and wonderful she couldn't tear her eyes from his strapping frame as he picked up the targets.

What was she supposed to do? A sharp longing for her mother and her sage advice gripped Jodie's insides, but on its heels a snippet from one of Mama's favorite hymns…

Take it to the Lord in prayer.

More of the song evaded her, but the message came through loud and clear. She latched onto the suggestion.

God, I'm in over my head. Show me what to do, please.

She'd no more than said "amen" when a calm washed away her worry, and in its place came the impression to wait. An odd notion, given that her days were numbered, but considering that she hadn't any better ideas, she opted to heed the advice.

After placing the hammer on an empty chamber, she set the gun beside the extra box of bullets on the wagon bed, wandered to the tree trunk, and sat down to do just that.

Leaving a loaded gun with a bandit probably wasn't the wisest thing Beau'd ever done, and not a mistake he planned to repeat, regardless of how beautiful or beguiling she was or how much he'd acted like a cad. Thankfully, Jodie didn't seem of a mind to use the weapon on him, idiot that he was. Because no lawman worth his salt would fall for a prisoner's feminine wiles. He could almost hear Uncle Beau, or at least his father, berating him. He had to do better at this job, and that meant no distractions and definitely no falling for the prisoner he guarded. Why did his first jailbird have to be a woman?

Women were completely and inexcusably nothing but trouble. They never took what he said in the manner it was meant, they always assumed the worst, and they never, ever considered how their laughter affected a guy's confidence. Just once he'd love to find a woman who believed in him and cared enough to look past his faults to see his heart. Surely there was a woman like that out there somewhere. After all, Texas was a mighty big place.

Knowing his luck, she probably didn't live in Texas though. If he couldn't find such a gal in a bustling city like San Antonio, he highly doubted he'd find such a woman in tiny Small Tree.

God, can't You take pity on this man?

Picking up the last tin can, Beau faced the wagon. *Might as well get this over with.*

He wandered back to the wagon, only to find Jodie reclined against the wide base of the spreading oak, her eyes closed in slumber, reminding him of how she'd looked yesterday morning in the cell. On the tails of that memory came the recollection of how she'd reacted to being awakened.

No woman should have that kind of gut reflex, outlaw or no. Why hadn't her brother protected her from such ill treatment? Better still, why had he dragged her into such a life in the first place? Had Jodie actually been a willing participant in his unlawful acts?

Lifting his hat, Beau swiped a sleeve across his brow, then resettled it and rested both palms on the wagon bed, his eyes landing on the revolver. With a sigh, he looked over his shoulder at his sleeping teacher. He'd only known Jodie for a short while, but the longer he knew her the harder it was for him to view her as an outlaw. His near-kiss earlier was a loud testimony to that. The woman was easy on the eyes, well put together, no denying that, but if he was honest, that wasn't all that made her attractive. This woman might've done bad things, might be a little rough around the edges, but there was a goodness in her he couldn't miss.

Would the judge miss it? Would he only see what she, or rather, what her brother's gang had done, or would the judge dig for the heart of the matter, the instigator of the crime? Leaning his back against the wagon, Beau nudged up his Stetson and rubbed at the tension building in his temples.

As marshal, didn't it fall on him to make sure the right person paid the penalty? Yes, Jodie was guilty of being a part of a gang. Yes, she was present at the explosion. Yes, she'd had goods from the mercantile in her possession, but had he ever stopped to ask how she'd come to have those goods? Had he ever asked how she'd come to be a part of that gang or what function she played in it?

He needed to know the truth. After all, the truth set people free.

Chapter 7

W e need to talk."

Jodie tore her attention from the exciting account of David versus Goliath and shifted her gaze to the marshal. The light from the oil lamp accentuated his striking features. Why hadn't he kissed her?

Shoving the better-left-unasked question aside, she marked her spot with her finger and closed the Bible. "We do?"

He'd hardly spoken to her since they'd left their shortened target practice. That he'd had a lot on his mind had been apparent with the way he'd scoured the papers on his desk. Either that or he was making an elaborate show of avoiding her. His current willingness to talk hopefully meant the former.

He looked at the sheet he'd been scribbling on since he'd locked her back in her cell. "We do."

"Okay." Jodie slipped the Bible's ribbon into place and gave him her full attention.

Beau sat in a chair right outside the bars so close she could see the ink smudges on his fingertips. With his leg bouncing, he glanced between her and what had to be his notes, his face a study in seriousness.

"Somethin's wrong. What is it?"

He rubbed the twin lines between his dark brows, leaving an adorable smudge, then dropped his hand to his lap with a sigh. "I'm not good at talking to women."

"You're doin' a pretty good job of it right now."

"Seriously. I—I sometimes stutter or...or things don't come out right and I make them mad."

"I won't get upset."

"You say that now."

"I promise. Just pretend I'm a guy and tell me what's on your mind."

His gaze swept over her from baggy shirt to broadcloth breeches before returning to her face. "Th–that's not possible."

Squelching the delight that rose up within her, she tried to think of another solution. "Would it help if I turned around?"

"I thought about that, but I need to see your face." He drew a deep breath and focused on the paper he repeatedly smoothed over his knee. "Let's just get this over with... I... *ahem*... The judge will be here in two weeks. We need to have a plan of how to present your case."

"My case? Wait. Did ya just say *we*?"

His movements stilling, he met her gaze head on. "I want to help you, Jodie, but I need to know the truth. About everything."

She opened her mouth to ask *why* but decided not to look a gift horse in the mouth. He wanted to help her, and she wasn't in any position to refuse. She doubted anyone else in this town would feel so kindly toward her.

"Everything? From the day of the robbery?"

"That's a start, but the more I know the better prepared I'll be to help you."

"You talk like you've done this kinda thing before."

"Not exactly. Let's just say my family has made it their business to know a thing or two about the law."

Which could mean any of a half dozen things.

His hand brushed hers, snatching her breath and her attention. "Trust me. Please. I won't let you down."

After a moment of consideration, she consented with a nod. Pulling away from his touch so she could think, Jodie drew a deep breath and gathered her thoughts.

"I hardly knew my brother before my parents died and I went to live with him. Jerry's fourteen years older than me, so he seemed more of an uncle than a brother. We got along pretty well. He taught me lots of things Mama never would've allowed, like shootin', 'n' trappin', 'n' fishin'—things I really enjoyed. Only after I got good at it, he started takin' trips for work. I hated it. He always left me behind. He said a neighbor would check on me, but they hardly ever did. He'd leave me alone in our cabin for days, then sometimes weeks at a time."

"How old were you?"

"About ten." Her mind went back to that last time he'd left her alone in their shack in the woods. Jerry'd promised to be home for Christmas. He'd already been gone five weeks, his longest absence yet. When Christmas came and went without seeing hide nor hair of him, she'd begun to wonder if something bad had happened, if God had taken him too, leaving her well and truly alone in the world.

Winter had whipped in sudden-like upon her, gripping the world in frost. Her supply of food and firewood dangerously low, she'd had to scrounge for fallen branches and dry brush to keep the hearth burning, divvying up what meager vegetables she'd stored and fishing for more meat. Some days she'd skipped meals to make sure she'd have enough for the next day.

"I'm sorry."

Jodie blinked, her gaze slipping from the past to the man outside the bars. "Yeah, well, finally, after one long absence, I told Jerry I'd had enough. I was through stayin' by myself and was goin' with him whether he liked it or not." Surely them being together was better than being alone. Although right now Jodie wasn't as confident of that.

"You didn't have any other relatives?"

"None that I know of." Jodie pulled her knees up to her chest and leaned against the cool brick wall. "Besides, I liked Jerry. He always made everything excitin'." Avoiding Beau's gaze, she rubbed at a stain on her breeches, much like the one God had scrubbed from her soul.

With sudden urgency, she gripped her knees and stared at Beau. "I swear I had no idea Jerry was hurtin' people. When I finally found out what he did for a livin', he told me they only took from those who could afford it so they could help the less fortunate, like Robin Hood. He convinced me we weren't doin' nothin' wrong, but…" She turned her head aside, unable to watch Beau's reaction to the rest. "I realize now the only one I was foolin' was myself. I–I wanted to believe we were helpin' folks, but lookin' back, I…I was the only one who ever gave any of our spoils away."

"So you participated in other raids?"

She wasn't sure how he kept the contempt out of his voice. "Not like the men. Before this last time, I only held the horses and kept watch. I just cooked 'n' cleaned 'n' looked after the supplies."

"Why the change?"

"I…I'm not sure. Maybe Jerry was afraid I'd do somethin' stupid."

"Like?"

"I don't know. Run away?" She finally looked at Beau, relieved to see his open expression hadn't changed. Why, only Heaven knew, but she leaned forward, eager for him to understand. "I think Jerry sensed my restlessness, that I was tired of livin' in the woods and wanderin' hither and yon, tired of dealin' with the others in the gang. I wanted out. I just hadn't been brave enough to tell him. Besides, it wasn't like I had anywhere else to go."

Leaning back against the wall, she breathed a sigh. If only she'd acted sooner, she wouldn't be in such a mess. Maybe she could've even gotten Jerry to change his ways and come with her. Maybe she could've met a good man like Beau and had a chance at a home, a family—love. Now she'd do well to be put on a chain gang instead of the end of a rope.

Beau scratched his chin and returned his grip to his thighs. "So you never actually stole anything?"

Frowning, Jodie considered his question. "I…Only what Jerry gave me. But I knew "

"And the goods from the store here in town—were you the one to carry them out?"

What was he getting at? "No, Jerry did, but—"

"Did you shoot at anyone?"

"No."

"So, your gun should be clean?"

"Of course." Finally catching his drift, Jodie stared wide-eyed at the man in front of her. "You think you can get me out of this alive."

"I'm no lawyer, but...I think so. On the Wanted poster I found, there's not a description of a young boy being in the gang, and definitely no description of a beautiful woman."

He thought her beautiful? Wait. "My brother's wanted?"

"Yes and his gang of *two* men."

"But I just told you—"

"That you cooked and cleaned and suffered the advances of such men."

"But I—"

"I'm not discounting what you've done, Jodie. Yes, you knew better, but you said yourself you wanted out. Not to mention, I highly doubt anyone would begrudge a child not wanting to be left alone. If you'll tell the judge all that and where to find your brother, I'm sure he'll go lenient on you."

Her rising hope plummeted. "You want me to rat out my own brother?"

Feeling a bit like a rat himself, Beau leaned forward, gentling his voice. "I know I'm asking a lot, but I don't see any other alternative." The woman in front of him looked away, making it slightly easier to say how he truly felt. "Please, Jodie. I... I want to see you get a second chance."

"I do too, but I...I'm not sure I can do that." She turned her head, allowing him to see the anguish in her blue-eyed gaze. "You have brothers. Would ya throw one of them to the wolves to save your own hide?"

As much as he disliked his brothers at times, the answer came easy. "No… I wouldn't."

"Then please don't ask me to do that. There's got to be another way. Wouldn't my testimony be enough? You said the judge wouldn't hold my choices as a child against me."

"I believe most wouldn't, but without some show of good faith, some proof that you truly desire to change, it's all dependent on your word. I can't guarantee that'll be enough for the judge."

"A show of good faith?" Jodie scooted forward and put her boots back on the floor. "What if I helped repair the damage at the mercantile, worked off the debt?"

Scratching his chin, Beau leaned against the chair back. "That, uh, that might actually help. Do you know anything about carpentry?"

"Well, not really, but I'm a quick learner, and if that doesn't work, maybe I could help restock the shelves or somethin'." She straightened, her countenance brightening. "And you could take me to church on Sundays. That'd surely say somethin'."

"I, uh, that's not a bad idea. Let me talk to a few people in the morning, and I'll see what I can arrange."

Jodie offered him a grateful smile, making him feel ten feet tall and bulletproof. He sure hoped this worked.

Jodie worked to hold the length of wood steady while Beau nailed the shelf's support on the other end. "You didn't have to do this."

"Do what?"

"Help."

The marshal withdrew another nail from his back pocket and positioned it against the two-inch-thick strip of wood. "I promised Haskins I'd keep an eye on you. I might as well make myself useful."

"I know, but this isn't your debt to pay."

Lowering the hammer, his gaze connected with hers. "I want to help you."

The way he said those words sent warmth spreading through her middle. "Thank you."

With a nod, he finished sinking the nail in place, then moved to her end. Grasping the brace near her hand, he held it against the wall. "Set that marble on the middle of the board, please."

Jodie did as requested and watched him nudge the wood up and down until the glass ball quit rolling and the board was level. "Hey, that's pretty smart. Where'd ya learn that trick?"

"I did some work once with an elderly carpenter who was going blind. He taught me." Beau tossed her a grin and held out his palm. "Now you're sworn to secrecy."

"My lips are sealed." Grinning back, she handed him a nail. "Why aren't you still workin' for him? You didn't want to be a carpenter?"

"I don't know." He tapped the nail into place and scooted down the board. "Mr. White died shortly thereafter."

Enjoying the easy way he talked to her while his mind was occupied with something else, Jodie handed him another nail. "Did you find another carpenter to work with?"

The nail disappeared into the wood. "No, a bricklayer."

"Oh." The marshal was beginning to sound like a jack-of-all-trades. "So why aren't you buildin' houses?"

"The man and his family decided to move to Colorado."

"And you didn't want to move."

"My folks wanted me to finish my schooling." Grabbing more nails, he continued down the narrow strip, anchoring it to the wall.

"Oh. So what else have you done?"

He took a few more nails in hand. "Umm... I've worked for an attorney"—*bam, bam*—"a house mover"—*bam, bam*—"a mercantile owner"—*bam, bam*—"even a flag maker." He motioned to the foot-wide board on the floor.

She grabbed the other end, helping him lift it into place on the anchored strip of wood.

"Do you have that while I nail this down?"

"I've got it." Making sure the wood plank stayed balanced on the oak strip and pressed against the wall while he nailed, Jodie commented on his recent job choice. "So, now you figured you'd try your hand at bein' a marshal?"

"I didn't plan on this job, didn't even ask for it, but it's growing on me." He drove a nail through the plank into the strip on the wall. "I enjoy helping folks."

Which somewhat explained his desire to help her.

Reaching over her shoulder, he readied another nail against the board and lifted the hammer.

Finding it hard to breathe, to think, with him so close, Jodie said the first thing to reach her lips. "I'm glad."

Warm air tickled her neck, raising gooseflesh on her arms. "I am too."

"Really?" She turned her head to read the truth in his coffee-colored gaze, only to find his face mere inches away.

"Really." His gaze traveled over her face, ending on her

lips.

Would he kiss her this time?

He leaned forward.

"How's it going back here?"

At Haskins's voice, Beau's head whipped toward the curtain-covered doorway, and Jodie's face flamed. Tucking her cheek against her shoulder, she pretended to be engrossed in holding the board, which could probably hold itself now.

"Uh, just fine." Beau smacked the nail into the wood, grunting as he nicked his thumb, and quickly stepped away. "Almost done with our second shelf." He tucked his injured thumb inside his fist and stashed it behind his back. "How are you liking the looks of things?"

"Are you sure it's gonna hold the weight of my merchandise? Looks kinda flimsy to me."

"It'll hold *me* when we get done."

"See that it does." With a frown, Haskins shifted his glare to her. "And see that none of my stuff goes missing while he's in here."

"I promise you, sir, you've nothing to worry about."

"Yeah, well—" The tinkling of the bell above the front door stopped the shopkeeper's next scathing remark. "I'll be back."

Jodie breathed a sigh when the crotchety man left the room, and sent Beau a concerned look. Would this show of good faith really be enough?

"We're gonna try somethin' different this time."

Beau sent Jodie a concerned glance, wondering what kind of creative lesson she had for him that day. The last two target practice sessions hadn't gone well. In fact, they'd been nothing more than a waste of time. He'd begun to wonder if it was possible to be a good lawman and not be able to hit the broad side of a barn.

"We're gonna take turns," Jodie continued. "While I shoot, you're gonna tell me a story, and while you shoot, I'll tell you one."

"A story?" He didn't see how storytelling was going to help his aim.

"Yes. Any kind of story ya want. About your childhood, your family, former jobs—you name it. Oh, and here, don't forget this." She flicked a dime his way.

He caught the coin in midair. "How is this supposed to help?"

"Remember, you balance the dime as you shoot to help steady your aim."

"I know about the dime. I meant the storytelling."

"I know." Grinning, she snapped the loaded cylinder closed and spun it. "Humor me. I want to see somethin'."

"Fine. Uh, who goes first?"

"Your choice."

Curious about what story she'd come up with, he lifted the pistol from her palm. "I guess I will."

"Okay." Jodie trailed behind him until they were a short distance from the wagon and stood opposite the targets. "Let's see. Oh, I know. There was this one time when I was a kid. I think I was about five or six. Papa was out workin', and I was helpin' Mama in the garden. She sent me to fetch water from the creek, and I found a stray dog hidin' in the bushes."

"It didn't attack you, did it?"

"Oh no. He was real friendly, but he was about the size of

57

a small horse. Or at least he seemed so to me, and I could tell he was hungry. So I decided to do somethin' about it. I led him back to the house, and while Mama was busy outside, I took him to the kitchen."

Grinning, Beau put the dime in place. He could see where this was going.

"I've never been very tall, so I couldn't reach much in the kitchen. But I could reach the egg basket on the table. I wasn't allowed to help at the stove without Mama, so I cracked some eggs in a bowl and scrambled them. I didn't know dogs shouldn't eat at the table, so I coaxed the critter up onto a chair."

Beau shook his head as he took aim.

"Needless to say, Mama came in about the time the dog had its dirty paws perched on the tabletop and was lickin' the last of the egg off her clean table. You'd think the roof'd caved in she put up such a racket. She took up a broom and went to squealin' and shoutin' at that dog so much Daddy came a runnin' in from the field to see what was wrong. He burst through the door, and the dog was in such a fever to get out of there, he knocked Daddy down in his haste. Mama ended up whackin' Daddy on the head, swattin' one last time at the dog."

Beau joined in Jodie's laughter, then steadied his aim and fired.

The tin can spiraled into the air.

With a shout, he turned to Jodie. "I did it!"

Her grin widened. "I figured you would once you stopped thinkin' so much."

"Huh?"

"Yesterday, when we were workin' on the shelves, I noticed you relaxed more when your hands and mind were busy. You didn't become self-conscious or hit your thumb until Haskins interrupted. I figured the same might work out here." She tapped the brim of his hat. "Sometimes, Beau Bones, you think too much." Jabbing a thumb in the direction of the remaining cans, she ordered, "Try it again."

He resumed his stance. Three of the remaining four cans toppled off the log.

With a whoop, Beau snatched Jodie around the waist and spun her around. Laughing, he staggered to a halt, only then realizing the line he'd crossed in his excitement. Jodie stood inches away, her arms braced against his, blue eyes sparkling, inviting.

An acorn pinged off his hat.

Blinking back to his senses, he looked upward and gave God a silent thanks. Beau gave Jodie a final squeeze and released her. "Thanks for your help."

She ducked her head, tucking a strand back into her bonnet. "Glad to do it."

"It's, uh, your turn, right?"

"Um…yeah." Taking the gun, Jodie moved away, heading to the wagon, undoubtedly to reload the Peacemaker.

With a sigh, he lifted his hat and raked a hand through his hair. *God, what am I doing here? She's my prisoner.* He had to get this attraction under control. Jodie had enough on her plate without romance muddying the waters, and who was to say she even returned the feelings? No, he had to keep his distance. He would be her friend, her advocate. Nothing more.

Chapter 8

Dipping his hat against the setting sun, Beau continued his meandering trek around town. As with the times he'd done this before, he kept his eyes peeled for anything suspicious, anyone watching or paying too much attention to the jail or happenings around town. He still couldn't shake the itch that a jailbreak was in the works.

No one in their right minds would leave someone like Jodie behind, sister or no. Her gang had to be planning something.

Two men he didn't recognize dismounted and slipped into the saloon down the street.

It looked like a good time for Beau's nightly visit to remind Mr. Shirley to keep the uproar to a minimum. He'd already had to settle three minor fights in the two weeks since he'd become marshal. If it hadn't meant Jodie sharing a cell, he might've locked up a few of the troublemakers to sleep off their inebriated condition and perhaps rethink their misconduct. Instead, he'd settled for a stern warning that must've done some good, because the rabble-rousers had changed faces each time.

Beau wasn't kidding himself. He knew some of these men probably respected his name more than his person, and one day they would surely test him. For now he was thankful that day hadn't come.

As he stepped up onto the boardwalk in front of the establishment, Beau ducked his head and peered through a window's plate glass. The place had a good turnout, not surprising for a Saturday evening. Most appeared to be the normal cowboys from neighboring ranches who sought to spend their week's pay on the world's vain pursuits.

Beau edged to the doorway and, from the shadows, peered over the batwing doors. He finally spotted the pair sitting belly-up to the bar talking to the rotund proprietor. Both were sturdy, one with black hair and garb, the other with overly long brown locks that curled from beneath his battered Stetson. Although they donned an air of nonchalance, their eyes were much too watchful.

Taking a steadying breath, Beau pushed inside. Most paid him no heed. A few glanced his direction. Carlos Shirley frowned. Beau tried not to let their reactions faze him and continued his meandering walk to the bar.

"Evening, Mr. Shirley." He nodded to the dusty pair. "Gentlemen." Turning, he leaned his elbow against the scarred wood. "I see y'all are gearing up for a banner night."

Boisterous laughter erupted from the back corner as one

greenhorn patron spit and sputtered at the crowded table, earning many sound pats and slaps on the back.

"Don't worry, Marshal. I'll see things don't get outta hand. I ain't forgot yer warning."

"See that you don't." Beau settled his gaze on the pair. "I haven't seen you two before. Welcome to Small Tree."

The black-haired one lifted his glass in acknowledgment, but neither said a word.

"Are you planning on staying long?"

The "talkative" one of the duo tossed back the last of his drink and donned his battered hat. "Nope."

Beau hid a frown as the two made their exit. Ignoring Shirley's muttering about running off paying customers, he bid the man goodnight and followed the pair outside at a more sedate pace. By the time he slipped out the batwing doors, they'd sunk spur and galloped up the road away from town. Neither of their chestnut horses had a distinguishing mark between them.

Almost like they were doing their best to blend in.

To go unnoticed.

Which made Beau notice them all the more.

His nagging itch turned into all-out hives.

Jerry waited ten minutes from the last chime of the church bell, then nodded to his men. Sneaking from the cover of the trees, they slipped past the handful of horses dozing in the shade of the livery stable and peered down the dusty road dividing the town in two.

Empty. Just as he expected.

He smiled behind his bandanna. They'd silence Small

Tree's sorry excuse for a marshal, grab Jo, and be miles away before anyone was the wiser. With nervous energy pulsing through his system, Jerry darted across the street, Dix and Pat on his tail. Guns drawn, bandannas in place, they barged inside the jail.

And stopped short.

Empty?

Not what he expected at all. An itch settled between Jerry's shoulder blades as he scanned the barren office.

"Where's the marshal?" Pat questioned as Jerry strode to the cell.

Empty as well.

Things weren't going according to plan. He hated when things didn't go according to plan. "Jo's not here either. He must've moved her somewhere."

Was the numbskull guarding his sister not as stupid as he looked? Had he suspected a jailbreak? Were they being watched even as they spoke? "We gotta get outta here."

The men didn't have to be told twice. They made a beeline for the trees. When they were well enough away with no one following, Jerry brought them to a halt.

"Now what?" The irritation in Dix's voice was unmistakable. That the mostly silent man spoke at all touted his growing impatience with the situation. They'd never hung around one place for so long, and the lack of movement was eating at all of them. This setback didn't help.

"Let me think." Jerry paced across the small clearing and stared at the minnows darting around in the shallows of the creek. Where would they have taken Jo? Pat had said the trial was set for next Tuesday. Had they moved it to another town?

"I ain't gonna stick around here forever and get my neck

stretched for some female." Untying his horse from a branch, Pat tugged the bandanna from his face. "What if she decides to rat us out?"

"Jo wouldn't do that."

"Maybe not to you—you're her brother. But there ain't nuthin' keeping her from squealing on us." Pat shared a glance with Dix, whose grave expression sounded his agreement. "That marshal's up to something. I could see it in his eyes last night."

"Then all the more reason for us to get her outta there." Jerry closed the distance between them. "We need to find where they moved her. Check the saloon. Keep your ears to the ground and see what you can find out. I'll keep an eye on the jail. We'll meet back at the camp at sundown."

Maybe by then the pair would have cooled off, and they'd have more answers and could form a new plan.

***

Jodie shifted on the split-log bench in the crowded new church. One would think for a new building they'd've made it big enough to hold everyone with a little extra space. As it was, Beau's thigh was pressed against hers, adding to the heat and increasing her awareness of his presence, if that was even possible. If she thought the man was a good-looker in Levis and a vest, he was downright gorgeous in a three-piece suit and tie. God had surely outdone Himself on Beau Bones. And not just with his looks. She'd never met a man more trustworthy and respectable since her father had died.

A hush fell over the room, drawing her attention to the front, where Reverend Miller, with his lanky stature and large nose, was taking his place behind the podium. Poor man put her in mind of an eel she'd once caught while fishing for supper. Thankfully, he didn't have the temperament to match, definitely wasn't as slippery, and for a preacher, he sure was soft-spoken. Jodie had to strain to hear him from the back of the room.

"Today's reading is from Proverbs chapter 3, verses 27 through 31." He lifted his Bible higher. "Read along with me. 'Withhold not good from them to whom it is due, when it is in the power of thine hand to do it.' "

Jodie shifted in her seat, wincing at the splinter that jabbed her backside almost as sharply as the verse stabbed her conscience.

" 'Say not unto thy neighbour, Go, and come again, and to morrow I will give; when thou hast it by thee. Devise not evil against thy neighbour, seeing he dwelleth securely by thee. Strive not with a man without cause, if he have done thee no harm.' "

Clutching her hands together, she resisted the urge to hide her face. How many times had she been a part of her brother's scheming to do people wrong? Maybe not directly, but every time she didn't open her mouth, every time she turned a blind eye to his actions, she'd contributed to his plans to harm others without cause.

" 'Envy thou not the oppressor, and choose none of his ways.' " The preacher closed his Bible, placing it back on the podium. "In this life, we all have choices. Some are easy. Some are hard. Sometimes we think making no choice will save us from the consequences, but making no choice is a choice in and of itself. We either choose to follow God and His ways or we don't. There is no middle ground."

Jodie shifted again and avoided Beau's gaze when he

glanced her direction.

"When we have the opportunity to do good," the preacher continued, "we shouldn't wait for someone else to do it or for a better time. We should follow God's leading and do as Jesus would. You may ask, 'How do I know what Jesus would do?' Ask yourself, 'What would love do?' in the situation. If it was your child asking for help and not a stranger, would you lend a hand? If it was you stuck on the side of the road in the rain with a broken axle, what would you want a passerby to do?

"Sometimes love requires getting messy. Sometimes it requires our time. Sometimes our goods or money. But when something is done from a heart of love, it will make a much bigger impact for the kingdom of God than something done out of compulsion. As we leave this place today, consider those around you. Look for opportunities to make a difference. Is there good you are withholding?"

The preacher bowed his head in prayer, but Jodie didn't move. She couldn't move as his final question echoed in her soul, eating at her calm. *God, are You trying to tell me to give up my brother's location?*

"So, what did you think of church?" Beau questioned as he slid tin cans on the top shelves in the mercantile storage room. Jodie had been quiet ever since they'd left the service two days ago, and her continued silence was making him nervous.

She paused in piling bolts of fabric on another shelf. "Huh? Oh, it was fine. I enjoyed the singin'."

So it must've been something in the sermon that was bothering her. "Reverend Miller delivered quite a message, didn't he?"

"Mmm."

He finished emptying his hands and turned to study her. "If you want to talk about it, I'll try to help."

She continued stacking items and emptying crates onto the shelves. As her silence lengthened, he resumed his work alongside her.

After some time, a sigh turned his head.

Jodie stood, head bowed, her hands gripping the edge of a shelf. "Do you think he's right?"

"Pardon?"

Rotating around, she leaned her back against the shelf and folded her arms. "Do you think the preacher was right?"

"About which part?" He shoved a barrel against the wall near her.

"The part about not withholding good."

"You mean the verse out of Proverbs 3? 'Withhold not good from them to whom it is due, when it is in the power of thine hand to do it'?"

"Yeah." Her head hung lower. "That part."

Scratching his neck, he leaned against the shelf beside her. "You're wondering if withholding the information about your brother's whereabouts is withholding good from the towns-folk, aren't you?" He hadn't realized until now that's where her mind had been, but he could see that being quite a dilemma.

Jodie rubbed at the creases in her brow. "If I tell y'all where he is, it'll do y'all good, but not him."

"Are you sure about that?"

"What?" She sought his gaze.

"Think about it. Has it done you good to get caught?"

"I...I suppose it has, but Jerry won't see it that way."

"If memory serves me correctly, you didn't see it that way at first either. In fact, I seem to recall some kicking and biting and *yelling*."

A hint of a smile curved her mouth for a brief moment then fell prey to the worry in her pale eyes. "But what if there's a shootout? I can't be responsible for my brother's death. He's the only family I got left."

Unable to resist the cry for help in her gaze, Beau slipped a supportive arm around her shoulders and squeezed. He wished he could shoulder this burden for her, make this easier, but some things only God could help with.

"I know it's not an easy decision to make, Jodie, but God will show you what's right. Why don't we pray for His help right now?" Relishing the feel of her at his side even though he knew he shouldn't, Beau bowed his head.

Jodie relished the feel of Beau's arm around her. No one had comforted her in such a way since her parents died. Jerry sure wasn't the demonstrative type. Bowing her head, she couldn't help leaning into the strong man beside her and wondering what it would be like to have his support all the time. Someone to pray with, talk to, and share her troubles. Someone who knew her faults but didn't shun her. But as her mama would say, if wishes were horses, everyone would ride.

"Father God..."

Jodie reined in her wandering thoughts and focused on Beau's prayer.

"You see Jodie's situation, her dilemma. This isn't an easy decision, but she wants to do what's right. I know that makes You proud. Show her, Lord, the way in which to go. Give her wisdom and the strength to do what You want her to do. Help everything to go well next week, better than we could imagine. In Jesus' name, amen." With a final squeeze, he slowly removed his arm.

She missed it immediately. "Thank you."

"Anytime."

The sincerity in his dark eyes tugged at her insides.

He touched her hand, as if he too longed to keep the connection alive between them. "You might try reading all of Proverbs 3, especially verses 5 and 6. They've helped me many times when I haven't known what to do."

"Okay."

"And if you ever want to talk…"

She squeezed his hand. "Thanks, Beau."

Chapter 9

Soft daylight crept through the bars above Jodie's head, marking the passing of another sleepless night. Another night without a peep from her brother. Another night without a single notion of how to deal with the verses from Proverbs 3. Another night of pondering more and more questions than answers. With a yawn, she rubbed at the tension between her eyes, then rested her cheek against her bent knees.

She'd been so certain Jerry would come for her, but it was becoming apparent she was guarding a man who didn't care to risk his neck for hers. She might as well accept the fact she was in this alone.

"I am with you always."

Too exhausted to be startled by God's whisper in her heart, she lifted her eyes to the window. *God, I'm a mess. Why do You waste time on me?*

"I have loved you with an everlasting love."

Hugging her knees, she closed her eyes and welcomed the comfort. *God, what do I do about Jerry? He's not ready to face You or a judge, but I don't want to die. I don't want to go to prison. I want a second chance to do things right.*

Wasn't that what her quandary all boiled down to? She wanted to do what was right but wasn't sure what *right* was. Was that turning in her only kin or showing him mercy? Betraying her brother or allowing him to go on hurting folks, to go on taking from those who'd done nothing to deserve such treatment? What was right? What was good?

She knew what Beau wanted. She knew what the town wanted. But what did God want? Opening the Bible on the blanket at her feet, she angled the pages toward the meager sunlight and reread the verses in Proverbs 3, starting at the beginning.

"My son, forget not my law; but let thine heart keep my commandments: for length of days, and long life, and peace, shall they add to thee." Long life. Peace. She surely wanted both of those.

"Let not mercy and truth forsake thee: bind them about thy neck; write them upon the table of thine heart: so shalt thou find favour and good understanding in the sight of God and man."

She could definitely use some favor, but if she showed her brother mercy, would she be forsaking telling the truth?

"Trust in the Lord with all thine heart; and lean not unto thine own understanding. In all thy ways acknowledge him, and he shall direct thy paths. Be not wise in thine own eyes: fear the Lord, and depart from evil."

With a sigh, Jodie bowed her head. Did she trust God? Really trust God? Enough to let go of what she wanted to happen and allow God to direct her? Maybe that's why direction seemed so fuzzy—she was too busy trying to make things go her way.

God, I give up. You know what's best for Jerry, and You know what's best for me. I trust that You'll do right by us both. If I need to speak with Beau about the rendezvous point, then give me the opportunity. If I need to remain silent, then help me to know that and to do so with a peace that comes only from You. Show me what I need to do, and give me the strength to follow Your lead...whatever that may be.

From his seat behind his uncle's desk, Beau gazed at the woman sleeping peacefully in the jail cell. After listening to her restlessness the past few nights, a part of him was relieved to see her finally resting. He could only hope that meant she'd come to a decision. What that decision was he had no idea. Would she finally reveal her brother's location, or had she decided to face the judge's verdict without that admission in her favor? He honestly couldn't blame her either way. He'd be hard-pressed to betray one of his brothers, no matter how much they'd teased and tortured him in the past. Family protected family.

A bird twittered outside the window, and the ticking clock on the opposite wall filled the silence of the late morning. Time was running out. If only he could think of something else to do to help Jodie, to guarantee her freedom. He couldn't stand to think of what would happen if he failed. Jodie didn't deserve to pay for her brother's crimes, for her decisions as a starving, lonely child. She deserved to have a second chance, to have a real life. A life with love and laughter and… Oh, he might as well admit it—he wanted her to have a life with him.

Jodie was a special woman. She had character, and he could see her growing in God and integrity every day. How could he get that across to the judge? He didn't know anything about Judge Johnson. If only he did. Maybe he should send a message to one of his brothers, see what he could find out. As soon as he considered the thought, he dismissed it. No, he needed to do this on his own. Well, not completely on his own.

God, please help us.

Jodie's fate would be decided in a matter of days, and in a way, so would his. Life wouldn't be the same without her. Not only that, but if he couldn't get her to give up her gang, would the town force him to give up his new job? A job he'd actually come to enjoy and wouldn't mind keeping. When they heard him fighting for her freedom in court, would they consider hiring him a mistake and send him packing? He didn't want to return home a failure again, but what else could he do? Jodie's brother was the true guilty party.

God, please don't let the wrong person be punished here.

Jodie shifted on her bunk, drawing his attention. Striped sunlight angled across her features, highlighting the delicate turn of her nose and chin, the soft curve of her cheek. Even in her patched, baggy clothes, her beauty shined. He couldn't believe how blind he'd been upon their first meeting. That just proved people normally saw what they wanted to see.

The words, *"Help them see,"* whispered across his heart.

Beau propped his head in his hands. *How, God?*

He already planned to reveal she was a woman, to have her share her story of the past, and to show the work she'd done toward restitution. Without the true guilty parties present, what more could he do?

An odd case his oldest brother had related to him awhile back surfaced in his mind.

God, is that You?

The idea was outlandish. Crazy even. Completely unlike him. But just crazy enough it might be God—and it might work. If the judge went for it. And Jodie.

He stared at the woman in the cell, the idea growing on him until a smile tugged on his lips.

Yes, it just might work.

"Jodie, I, uh, wondered if we could talk?"

Jodie stilled at Beau's question. So that's the way it was to be. Dawn barely even hinted outside her window, and God was already supplying her with an answer. With a nod, she set aside the towel she'd been drying her face on and moved to take a seat on the bunk.

"No, out here." Beau unlocked the cell.

Surprised, Jodie changed course and followed him to the chairs in front of the desk. Warm lantern light pushed back the predawn darkness but did nothing to settle the swirl of nervous grasshoppers that took to hopping in her gut.

She perched on the edge of her seat and gripped the sides. "I have something I want to talk to you about too, but you first."

"All right." He settled on the chair in front of her and rubbed his legs. "Look, I know you've been struggling over what to do about your brother."

She nodded. Peace had alluded her until she'd surrendered to God early yesterday morning. She was acutely aware that they were less than three days from the trial. Unfortunately, her brother might not even be in the area anymore.

"Well, I, uh… I, uh…"

Clearly she wasn't the only one unsettled by this conversation. Swallowing a smile, she stilled Beau's sliding hand with a touch.

"It's me, Beau. Just tell me whatever it is you're thinkin'."

He turned his hand to grip hers. "Look, I, uh… I had an idea come to mind yesterday while I was watching you sleep. I–I mean, while you were sleeping. I–I mean I was watching you, but that is… I mean…not like…" Ducking his head, he used his free hand to rake through his already tousled hair.

Her smile broke free at how completely adorable he was when he got flustered. "What was your idea?"

"We're friends, right? I mean, you like me? I'm not completely abhorrent to you?"

"Of course you're not. What kind of question is that? You're the best friend I've ever had."

"Good." With a deep exhale, a wave of his nervousness seemed to wash away. "Good. Because I thought of this old ca—"

The door slammed open, wood splintering from the frame.

With a hard yank, Jodie carried Beau to the floor between the chairs.

Two men stepped into the room, their hard soles thudding against the planks.

"We've c— What's goin' on here?"

At the familiar voice, Jodie jerked her gaze up to find her

brother standing not three feet away.
    With his gun barrel aimed at Beau's head.

Chapter 10

B eau's blood ran cold at the sight of the six-shooter aimed their direction, but instead of freezing him, the chill cleared his head. Snapping upright, he shoved Jodie behind him and darted a glance at his gun belt hanging on the hat rack behind the desk.

"I wouldn't try it, mister." The second man, stout like the "talkative" one from the saloon with eyes as black as sin above a dark bandanna, leveled a second gun on him.

"Come on, Jo." The first man barked the order, his dark hair and pale eyes a testament of his identity. The light blue color that was fetching on Jodie looked more like frigid ice on this fellow.

Jodie didn't move, except to tighten her grip on Beau's arm. "You don't have to do this, Jerry. I'm okay. If you'd just give these people back—"

"Quit wastin' time 'n' come on."

The pressure on his arm shifted, and Beau felt Jodie rise.

"I–I'm not goin' with you."

"*What?*" the second man exclaimed.

Jerry's eyes widened then narrowed. "Quit your foolin', Jo, 'n' get over here. We ain't got time for your nonsense."

"It's not nonsense. What you're doin' is wrong, and I don't want to be part of it no more. Do ya think Mama and Papa would be proud of what you're doin'? That God's pl—"

"Enough!" Jerry raised a fist, clearly clinging to his calm by a thread. "Get over here. I ain't lettin' you hang for my crimes. Now come on."

Beau felt Jodie's gaze on him, but he didn't dare tear his focus away from that pistol. *God, help us.*

After a heartbeat of silence, a delicate hand slid onto his shoulder. "No, I'm stayin' with Beau."

Even as his chest expanded with pride and another emotion he couldn't name, Beau's heart skipped a beat as Jerry's countenance darkened.

"Beau, is it?" Her brother cocked a brow. "Well, I ain't leavin' here without you, and if he's the only thing standin' in your way…" His thumb pulled the cock back the full distance.

Beau's breathing ceased.

Jodie glanced back over her shoulder for one last peek of the marshal lying unconscious behind the bars a heartbeat before her brother dragged her the rest of the way out of the jail and tossed her into a saddle. "You didn't have to hit him."

Jerry swung onto his own mount. "He put his hands on

you."

"He was only protectin' me."

"So am I." Jerry kicked his horse into a gallop behind Dix and Pat.

When her horse quickly followed suit, Jodie realized her brother'd dropped a rope around her saddle horn.

As much as she wanted to slip the rope and turn around, she knew she couldn't, at least not yet. She had the sickening feeling if she tried to go back, if she fought her brother, he'd keep his threat to shoot the marshal. Something she couldn't let happen.

Seeing that gun aimed at Beau, she knew without a doubt that somewhere in the past month she'd fallen in love with him. It was ridiculous, a prisoner falling in love with the prison keeper, but she couldn't deny it. And that's why she'd had no other choice than to leave with her brother, even though every fiber of her being had wanted to stay. Beau knew that, and the look in his eyes before Jerry'd laid him flat said he wouldn't let her go without a fight. Or at least she hoped that's what that look meant.

God, what do I do?

Something banged against her leg. A bag. She pulled one of the straps off the saddle horn and squinted at the inside in the growing dawn. A money bag? Grinning, Jodie grabbed a handful of bills, then hesitated. Her brother would notice the missing bills quicker. She dug to the bottom of the bag and found a jumble of coins.

Leaning over the saddle, she draped her arm against her leg and dropped a coin…then another…then another, praying all the while Beau would find her trail and come to her rescue.

Before Jerry realized what she was doing.

With a groan, Beau sat up and rubbed his aching jaw. Opening his eyes, he took in his surroundings and scrambled to his feet. He gripped the bars on the door and yanked with all his might.

The metal only clanked together.

He had to get out of here. Jodie needed him. Shouting at the top of his lungs, he rattled the cell door. When that didn't summon anyone, he moved to the window that revealed the sun cresting the horizon. How long had he been out? "Help!"

He glanced around. The key, the key. Where was the key? There. On the desk. On the corner closest to him.

Surveying the cell, he tried to find something long enough to help him reach it. The bed frame was metal. That wouldn't work. Wait. He yanked the lumpy mattress onto the floor.

"Hallelujah." It was a rope bed, just as he'd hoped. Finding one end, he quickly untied the knot and began untangling the lattice work. Maybe all that time dealing with his brothers' shenanigans had been a good thing after all. Maybe God had been preparing him for this work all his life and he just hadn't known it. Maybe he'd finally found his place in this world. Now he just had to get back his woman.

The last of the rope slid free. Now to make a lasso. *Thank you, Austin.* Quickly forming a honda knot, he praised God his next-to-oldest brother had rebelled and gone through a cowboy phase he'd never grown out of. In no time at all, he had the lariat made and swinging on the outside of the bars.

Lord, guide my aim.

His first toss overshot the key ring, but as he reeled it in, the rope caught and dropped the ring to the floor. He just had to get it closer. He swung again, missed, and tried again. This time the loop surrounded the keys. *Yes!*

Beau gingerly drew the prize his way. When he could finally reach it, he snatched up the key and crammed it into the lock. He darted out, grabbing up his gun belt and some extra bullets before racing across the street where the livery man was just opening his door.

"Hewitt!"

The balding man swiveled his direction. "Marshal, what's wrong?"

"Saddle some horses. My prisoner's been kidnapped."

"A jailbreak?"

Beau didn't stop to explain. He continued down the street, shouting over his shoulder, "I'll be back shortly with more men."

"What is it, Lawson?" Beau watched the lanky man pick up something small and shiny from the dirt. Their posse of about a dozen men had split up, covering multiple directions, trying to find the gang's path on the hard, trampled ground. Beau had made sure to keep Lawson, the best tracker in the area, with him. Cyrus, a quiet crack shot, rounded out their small group.

"I'm not sure." The tanner stood, surveyed the area again, took a handful of steps down the road, and stooped once more. "If I didn't know any better, Marshal, I'd say we've got ourselves a money trail."

Beau swung down from the saddle and approached. "A money trail?"

Midday sunlight glinted off a penny and five-cent piece in the man's outstretched hand.

Cyrus meandered past them a short ways, glanced around, took a few more steps, knelt, and held up a half-dollar.

Jodie.

Hope sprang to life in Beau's chest. He hadn't lost her. "Where does this road lead?"

Lawson shoved the money into Beau's hand and reached for his saddle. "It splits not too far from here, going in multiple directions."

Which explained why the gang had chosen this path. Beau and Cyrus followed suit, remounting. "Any of those directions lead to a possible hideout?"

"More than one." Lawson kneed his horse, his attention on the ground. "Good thing your prisoner is showing us the way."

Keep it up, Jodie. I'm coming.

Chapter 11

Jodie breathed a sigh of relief when her brother called them to a stop. As if it too were exhausted, the sun propped itself on the horizon, lengthening the shadows and lessening its scalding touch. Moving gingerly, she climbed from the saddle and locked her knees to keep from sinking all the way to the ground. She hadn't ridden so long or so hard in many a day. They'd only stopped long enough to water or trade out horses, putting them miles from Small Tree and the marshal.

Needless to say, her backside hurt like nobody's business and she couldn't wait to fall into a bedroll. Slipping the few coins in her grip into her pocket, Jodie arched her back and twisted away some of the kinks.

"Get some supper goin'." Jerry tossed a saddlebag her direction.

She didn't even try to catch it. The flap popped open as it hit the dirt, sending potatoes spilling out onto her boots. Not ready to try her brother's temper in her current state, Jodie forced her limbs to move, scooped up the bag, and shuffled over to a gigantic boulder. Welcome blood returned to her extremities as she gathered sticks, built a campfire, and took stock of her supplies.

When she knelt to start slicing spuds, her knife froze over the first potato as a sudden thought struck—these were stolen potatoes, as were the ham and salt. She couldn't cook these. She glanced at her brother where he worked with the others rubbing down their horses. He'd be furious if she refused, but the only one around for him to threaten now was her, and he'd never hurt her. Maybe if he realized she'd changed, that she wasn't gonna go back to the way things were, maybe he'd let her go.

God, give me strength.

Emptying her hands, Jodie rose on unsteady legs. How did she tell the one who'd taken care of her for almost a decade that she didn't want to stay with him? *Thanks for all you've done for me, but I don't need you anymore.* Yeah, that would sit well.

God, what do I say? She rubbed her hands on her thighs and tried to summon up the words and the courage to move.

Jerry must've felt her gaze, because he looked her way before she was ready. "What's the matter?"

Stiffening her spine, she clenched her hands together. "Can we talk?"

"After supper." He turned away as the men led the other horses toward the creek trickling a short distance away.

"No." She held her breath, swallowing a gulp when he

looked back. "Before."

With a huff, he tossed the burlap bag by his saddle and stalked her direction. "What?"

"Jerry, I…" She glanced off, her focus falling on the food. Sighing, she looked back into eyes much like her own. "Jerry, while I was in jail, I…" She lifted her hands in a shrug. "I changed."

"You forgot how to cook?"

"No, I…I remembered." Shoving her hands in her pockets, her fingers collided with the last few coins. Was Beau nearby? Had he found her trail? Or was she in this alone?

"Lo, I am with you always."

That's right; she was never alone. God had promised never to leave her. Even if Beau never showed up, she could face the future, get a fresh start…with God. She straightened, relying on His strength to get her through this and all the days ahead.

"I remembered what it was like to be in one place for more than a week. I–I remembered the fun I used to have workin' alongside Mama and Papa. I remembered what it was like not havin' to constantly look over my shoulder. I remembered…" She reached out and touched her brother's arm. "I remembered God."

Jerry yanked away, but she had to give him credit for not stomping off.

"Or should I say He showed me that He hadn't forgotten about me. Jerry, we don't have to live like this."

"Oh, what am I supposed to do? Go traipsin' back to town and turn myself in to your beau?"

"Would that be so bad?"

With a shake of his head, Jerry walked a few steps away

and then stalked back. "They'll hang me. Is that what you want? Those people back there... they don't care one whit about folks changin'. They won't care if you've turned over a new leaf. All they'll see is what you've done, what I've done. They spout off a bunch of religious claptrap, but in the end all they want is your hide. Don't you see..." He gripped her arms. "There ain't no goin' back. They ain't gonna forget. They ain't gonna accept you. There ain't no happily-ever-afters in this life. Face it, Jo, there's no such thing as a second chance."

No such thing... Was what he said true? Would they not care about the good she'd done, the restitution she'd tried to make? Was it just wishful thinking to believe she could have a future? Would all her striving be for naught? Was there really no such thing as a second chance?

She paused, considering, then straightened, her resolve strengthening. "No. No, I refuse to believe that. God took me back. He'll take you back too."

"Ha. Even if He did, they ain't gonna forget what we've done. I ain't goin' back, Jo." Jerry turned and began walking away.

Swallowing the Texas-size lump in her throat, Jodie forced out the words, "And I ain't stayin'."

He stopped. After a moment, his shoulders lifted then sagged. "So be it." With a sad shake of his head, he continued walking toward the other men.

A twig snapped. A shotgun cocked.

Before Jodie could spot the source, Jerry took off running for his horse.

Bedlam erupted. Three men emerged from behind trees. Beau! Shouts. Scrambling. Whinnying. Pat vaulted onto a horse bareback. Beau landed a lasso around him, yanking him onto the creek bank.

A shot went off.

Jodie dropped to the dirt.

Beau peered about and spotted Jodie lying in the dirt near a saddlebag. His heart stopped. Shoving the rope into Cyrus's grip, Beau sprinted toward the woman he loved. In that moment, he couldn't deny it. He loved her. And if he'd found her only to lose her again, he didn't know what he'd do.

Please, God, no.

He dropped to his knees and grabbed her shoulder. "Jodie?" Rolling her over, he found tears streaking her cheeks. "Where are you hurt? Are you shot?" He scanned her form. No blood.

"I'm fine."

Thank God.

Swiping a hand over her face, she sat up. "Jerry left."

Beau surveyed the area in the waning twilight. Sure enough, her brother was missing. He didn't know whether to be relieved or upset.

"He wouldn't listen, Beau. I tried to get him to turn hisself in."

Pulling her into his arms, Beau tucked her head beneath his chin. "I know. I heard part of what you said. Don't worry. We'll find him." Although, for the sake of the woman in his hold, he wasn't sure how hard he'd look. With the other two gang members in custody, Jerry Ross would have to start from scratch, and hopefully the town would be satisfied enough with the other two to let Beau keep his job.

Leaning back, Jodie stared up at him. "Do you think he'll ever change?"

"If God can stop Paul and turn his heart around, He can get ahold of your brother. No doubt. We'll pray for him."

With a nod, Jodie leaned back into Beau's chest about the same time a throat cleared behind them.

"Uh, Marshal?" Lawson peered down at them with an odd expression.

"Oh." Beau pushed to his feet and helped Jodie to hers. "Mr. Lawson, I'd like you to meet *Miss* Jodie Ross, the *lady* who left you a shining trail."

"Lady?" After scanning the length of the dirt-coated woman, Lawson focused on her face. "Well, I'll be..." He glanced over his shoulder to where Cyrus held a gun on the pair of outlaws tied to a sturdy oak. "Hey, Cy. Come get a load of this. He's a she." Lawson's attention shifted back around. "You've been guarding a woman all this time? And the work at the mercantile... The missus is gonna hit the floor when she hears this one. Ma'am, that was a mighty brave thing you did, leaving us that trail. Made my job tracking y'all a whole lot easier."

"You'll be sure to tell that to the judge?" Beau questioned.

"Oh, yes, sir."

"Thank you, Mr. Lawson." Jodie smiled then peered up at Beau. "What now?"

Indeed, what now? Beau scanned the growing darkness. "I guess we'll camp here for the night and head back to town in the morning."

"What about Jerry?"

"I, uh..." Beau scratched his chin and glanced at Lawson. "You think you could find his trail in the dark?"

Lawson cocked his head in thought as he surveyed the area. "With us being so close to a creek, I've a feeling he pulled the same stunt he did back at Small Tree and traveled upstream a ways. Without a full moon, it'd be nigh unto impossible to find his exit point by lantern light, not to mention the risk to the horses."

The man had a very good point. "What about in the morning? We've got to get these men and Jodie back to town before the judge arrives."

"We can look, but I'd guess he'll be long gone by then."

Beau would be too if he were in Jerry's shoes. "Might be wiser to wire the sheriffs in the surrounding counties with his description and get these two behind bars."

"What you gonna do with Miss Ross here?"

Jodie shared an uncertain glance with him.

"I guess we'll figure that out when we get back to town."

After another day and a half on horseback, at a much slower pace, Jodie caught a glimpse of Small Tree in the distance. She shifted in her saddle. Did she really want to go through with this? Did she really want to risk facing a judge and whatever verdict he might render? Would it be better just to knee her horse and make a run for it? She glanced about and found Beau's gaze on her. For some reason, her insides calmed.

Beau nudged his mount and closed the gap between them at the front of their pack. "Having second thoughts?"

"No, I'm through with runnin'. Just a little worried about tomorrow." She turned her focus back on the town. "You think the judge has arrived yet?"

Peering upward, Beau took in the position of the sun.

"Possibly. Depends on if the stage is running late or not." He cleared his throat. "Jodie, before we were interrupted back at the jail, there was, uh, something I wanted to discuss with you."

"Yes?"

"I, uh…"

A shout and jangle of harnesses yanked their attention to the road behind them. The stage barreled their direction, the hooves of the six-horse team thundering against the hard-packed earth. Their group broke apart, moving to the grassy sides of the narrow road. As the red-and-yellow Wells Fargo coach hurried past, a man with a handlebar mustache and salt-and-pepper hair stuck his head out the window. His dark eyes widened, his focus fixed on them as he continued down the road.

Jodie glanced at Beau to find him wide-eyed, his mouth gaped slightly open. "Do you know who that was?"

Beau jerked at Jodie's question. Tearing his gaze away from the stagecoach's passenger, he looked across the road. "Lawson, I thought they said Judge Johnson was presiding over this case?"

"They did."

"Well, that's not who was on that stage." He kneed his horse into a gallop. This wasn't happening. He'd rather deal with a stranger presiding over Jodie's case. There's no telling what would happen now.

Then again, maybe he was wrong. Maybe his mother was just checking up on him. Maybe Judge Johnson really was on that stage. Maybe, just maybe, his eyes were deceiving him and that wasn't—

"Beau, what's wrong?" Jodie rode up beside him. "Who was that?"

Beau watched the stage rein to a stop in the middle of town. A heartbeat later, a well-dressed, well-groomed older gentleman disembarked and turned their direction, sending Beau's stomach plummeting. Even from this distance, there was no denying who'd come to town.

"My father."

Chapter 12

Jodie glanced between Beau and the distinguished-looking man across from him on the boardwalk and couldn't help but see the family resemblance. Both had strong cheekbones, a defined chin, straight nose, and dark eyes. However, the older gentleman had a presence that she could only describe as overpowering.

The men shook hands, Beau's normally congenial manner subdued. "Father, I didn't realize you were coming."

"Did not."

"I apologize. I *did not* realize you were coming. Did Mother send you?"

"No, Judge Johnson called upon me for my assistance since he is currently detained with another case and I was free for a few days. Your mother sends her regards though and wonders why you have not returned home yet."

"I see." Beau's Adam's apple bobbed. "I have, uh, taken a job here."

"Then it is not your uncle's affairs that have delayed your return?"

"Uh...not exactly." Beau shifted in his boots.

"Then what, *exactly*?"

"Hey, Marshal!" Lawson stopped his horse at the hitching rail across the street, the other three coming to a halt beside him. "You want us to take these two inside and lock them up for you?"

After a long blink, Beau turned to face Lawson. "Yeah, if you don't mind. I have some business to handle out here. Keep an eye on them for me until I get through, will you?"

"Sure. What you gonna do with her?"

Beau glanced Jodie's way, uncertainty covering his handsome features.

Before he could voice a word, she touched his arm and gave a small smile. "Don't worry. I don't mind waitin' with him."

She took a step toward the jail, but Beau's hand on hers stopped her progress. "Outside the cell. I don't want you in there with those two."

With a nod, she squeezed his fingers. "Okay."

"Marshal? Your job is the town *marshal*?"

Beau tried not to wince at his father's tone as Jodie slipped inside the jail. This might be the hardest conversation he'd ever had with his father, and he'd had quite a few. And tomorrow they'd meet each other in court. Wonderful. Why couldn't his life ever be easy?

Gathering his courage, Beau faced his father. "Yes, I'm the marshal. I have been for nearly a month now."

Father came as close to a public display of emotion as Beau had ever seen as he snagged Beau's arm and dragged him into the alley between the livery and feedstore. "Are you out of your mind? I wanted you to show interest in the law, but this... Your mother is going to have a fit of the vapors when she hears what you have been up to." He swiped his handkerchief across his face and began to pace. "And that woman, if you can even call her a woman in that outfit...."

His temperature spiking, Beau stiffened. "Mind what you say about Jodie, sir."

Father stopped mid-pace and stared at him, his graying brows winging upward then slamming low. "What did you say to me?"

"I don't want to fight with you, sir, but I won't have you speaking ill of Jodie. She just risked everything to bring those two outlaws you saw to justice."

His father looked at him askance, then gave a nod of acquiescence. "Fine, but you will give your resignation as marshal and return home with me as soon as this trial is over. Your position is still avail—"

"I'm not resigning." Beau wasn't sure where he got the courage to interrupt his father, but as long as he was being stupid, he might as well spit it all out. "I enjoy being the town marshal. Furthermore, I'm good at it."

"But you have never even fired a gun."

"Yes, I have, sir. Jodie taught me, and I've been practicing."

Father planted his hands on his hips and lowered his head.

After mumbling something under his breath, he gave a huff and met Beau's gaze. "I do not have time for this nonsense. I have accommodations to find and a trial for which to prepare."

"So do I. And I have wires to send."

"Fine. We will finish this discussion after the trial. Agreed?"

Beau wouldn't change his mind, but he nodded anyway. He dreaded tomorrow more than ever before.

Jodie smoothed a hand down the bluebonnet-colored dress she hadn't worn since the last time she and Beau had gone target practicing. Sitting in the middle of the wooden pew at the front of the schoolhouse, she felt about as conspicuous and perilous as one of those tin cans. Whispers surrounded her, and she could feel every stare centered on her. Why had she let Beau talk her into wearing this getup? She'd just have to change when his father sent her to the state prison.

Beau touched her hand, making her start. "It's going to be okay."

That's what he thought. She tossed a backward glance at the lanky man beside Dix and Pat, then whispered to Beau. "Lawson said Judge Bones is one of the hardest judges around."

"He is."

"Then how are you so calm?"

"Because the two truly guilty parties are sitting behind you."

Jodie peeked again at Dix and Pat, handcuffed and stuffed in the pew next to Lawson. Their hardened glares made her glad Beau had insisted on giving her his room last night and stayed at his desk to keep an eye on things.

A door beside the chalkboard at the front of the building opened, and Judge Bones stepped inside. Dread pooled in her stomach as a hush fell over the building and everyone rose to their feet until Beau's father took his seat.

The somber man set a gavel on the teacher's desk then took in the crowd gathered. When his focus landed on Jodie, clad in ribbons and lace, his gaze shot to his son.

"Who is the defendant? I was told the individual on trial was a"—he glanced at the paper in front of him—"Joe Ross."

Beau rose. "She's the defendant, Your Honor. Her name is Miss Jodie Ross."

"Jodie?" The judge's gaze flickered between the two of them, then leveled on his son.

"Yes, sir. Jodie. Jo for short. We believed her a man when she was arrested."

"Then you men need to get some spectacles. Young lady, are you telling me you were a part of the gang that robbed and blew up the general store?"

Jodie peered up at Beau, who gave her an encouraging nod, so she rose to stand beside him. "Yes, sir." She rotated slightly and gestured to the two men behind her. "Dix and Pat were the other two members in my brother's gang."

Murmuring ensued, quieted only by the judge's gavel.

"Am I also to believe you were instrumental in capturing these two men?"

"Yes, Your Honor." Jodie glanced at Beau, wondering if she should say more. At his nod, she added. "When my brother's gang broke me out of jail and forced me to go with them, I left a trail for the marshal and his men to follow."

Judge Bones sat back in his chair, his expression revealing little. "What kind of trail?"

"Coins, sir."

"Is this true?" The question was directed at Beau.

"Yes, Your Honor. With your permission, I would like Miss Ross to share her story with the court. I believe you will see she is a prime candidate for rehabilitation."

"We shall see. Continue, young lady."

After another encouraging nod from Beau, Jodie gathered her nerve, ignored the stares, and forced herself to tell everyone of her past—from her childhood to that day.

With as stoic a face as she'd ever seen, Judge Bones listened as she told of her part in her brother's gang, about the day of the general store robbery, and the day her brother kidnapped her from the jailhouse. He then shifted his attention to Beau. "Is there anything else you would like to add, Marshal?"

"Yes, Your Honor." Beau returned to his feet and shared about the times he'd found her reading the Bible, the work she'd done at the mercantile, and her request to attend services at the church. He then shared his account of the jailbreak and subsequent capture.

"I see, and you believe Miss Ross should be excused from serving time in prison for her crimes?"

Beau stiffened beside her. "I believe Miss Ross has demonstrated her desire to become a productive part of society, rather than to continue in her brother's unlawful footsteps, Your Honor."

"And you would have me simply release her on her own recognizance? That is not permissible. She must have a place of residence, a job in the community, and a guardian willing to take responsibility for her and her actions and to teach her to live within the bounds of society. Does she have these things?"

Jodie locked her knees to keep from wilting to her seat. She didn't have any of those. Prison. She was bound for prison. *God, give me strength.* Drawing a shaky breath, she forced herself to meet the judge's gaze. As she began to shake her head, Beau cleared his throat beside her.

"Actually, Your Honor, she does."

Jodie's gaze collided with Beau's. "I do?"

"She does?" The judge seemed equally shocked.

"Yes, sir." Beau drew a deep breath and straightened to his full height. "If Miss Ross is agreeable, she has a job waiting for her that also includes accommodations."

"And what job is that?"

Turning his focus on her, Beau offered a tentative smile. "The job of being my wife."

Jodie's gasp was echoed by the others present.

"*What?*" The judge's voice boomed to the rafters, the crowd joining in the uproar, but Jodie couldn't tear her gaze away from the man staring at her with an intensity that sent her pulse thrumming through her veins like a freight train. Was this really happening?

"Your wife? You want to marry me? You'd marry me just to keep me out of prison?"

Beau took a step toward her, closing the gap between them. "No."

Her thrumming freight train crashed. "But you just said..."

"I said I want to marry you, but it's not just to keep you out of prison."

"It's not?"

"No." Shaking his head, he lifted a thumb and traced her jawline, setting the fire from the crash spiriting through her veins. "It's because I don't want to let you out of my sight. I want to wake up with this beautiful face looking at me every morning and go to sleep with you resting beside me every night. I want to know you're safe and taken care of and to help all your dreams come true. I want *you*, Jodie Ross. I want you as my wife, because imagining a day without you is torture, and there's no one else I'd rather spend my life with. I…I love you."

Chapter 13

A ringing gavel and a shouting judge interrupted Jodie's response and sent silence pouring through the room as Judge Bones's threatening glare traveled the expanse, coming to rest on his son.

"Marshal Bones, a word…"

Before Beau could move, a throat cleared behind them, drawing everyone's attention to the center aisle where Mr. Haskins stood rotating his flat-brim straw hat in his hands.

"Your Honor, if I may, I have something to say."

"Who are you?"

"My name is Robert Haskins. I own the general store that was robbed." The bald man glanced Jodie's way with an indiscernible expression before looking back at the judge.

"Make it quick."

Haskins tugged at his vest and straightened. "Your Honor, I...I would like to drop the charges against Miss Ross."

A wave of shock rippled through Jodie and flowed through the crowd.

The judge silenced their murmurs with a bang of his gavel.

With another glance in her direction, Haskins continued. "Miss Ross isn't responsible for blowing up my store. Those other two men are. In fact..." Peering at his hat, Haskins rotated it in his wrinkled hands. "When I was coming to, I heard Miss Ross trying to talk her brother out of it."

The uproar and banging ensued again.

Ignoring the chaos, Jodie stared at the man offering her freedom. Why was he doing this?

As if in answer to her question, the crotchety old man continued, "Miss Ross paid for whatever part she played in her brother's crimes by helping rebuild and restock my shelves." He lifted his chin. "She deserves a second chance."

Jodie sat. Hard. Tears pricked her eyes. She knew Jerry'd been wrong.

The judge regained order, and with a final bang of his gavel, declared, "Case dismissed. Miss Ross, you are free to go. As for these other two men, we will deal with them this afternoon. Marshal Bones... a word."

Everything continued around Jodie in a haze. Free? Case dismissed? She wasn't going to prison? Her nightmare was over?

Beau gave her arm a parting squeeze. Why didn't he look happy? He said something to Lawson, pointing to Dix and Pat, then headed toward his father.

Jodie's gaze landed on Mr. Haskins, who was already

making tracks for the door. "Mr. Haskins." She stood and moved out of the pew, her voice growing in strength as the stunned haze lifted. "Mr. Haskins!"

Halfway across the schoolyard she caught up to him. "Mr. Haskins…" She caught his arm, forcing him to stop and face her. The same hard expression was firmly back in place, but this time she saw beneath the veneer. "Why?"

"Why what?"

"Why'd you do it? Why'd you stand up for me? I thought you hated me."

"You paid your time. Now don't make me regret it."

"I–I won't, but…"

Haskins's gaze lazily roamed over her face. After a moment, his veneer cracked, and he cupped her cheek. "You remind me so much of my daughter."

"I do?"

"If only I'd…" With a cough, he dropped his hand. "Yes, well… if you need a job, you come see me. Don't you let that marshal force you into marrying him if you don't want to."

"I, um…I won't. Thank you."

"Don't mention it. Ever." A quick pivot and the old codger stalked away, leaving Jodie staring after him.

A shout behind her drew her attention.

Beau.

She smiled. Then his words in the courtroom came slamming back through her. Beau? What on earth was she going to say to him?

Beau hurried to close the distance between himself and Jodie. Curious eyes followed his progress, but for once, he didn't care. He had to know how Jodie was faring. What had Haskins said to her? Had she given any thought to his proposal?

"Jodie…" He cupped her arms. "Are you okay? I saw you talking to Haskins."

"I'm, uh, I'm fine. He, uh…he offered me a job." Avoiding his gaze, she stared at his hand on her arm.

Did she want him to let go? Had he acted too rashly and lost her? Messed up like he had with every other woman he'd taken a chance to get to know? "Wh–what did you tell him?"

"I…thanked him." She still wouldn't look at him.

It was true; he'd lost her. He dropped his arms to his sides, releasing her. Why did he always mess these things up? What was wrong with him? He thought he'd finally found the one gal who looked past his faults, who understood him. He raked a hand through his hair. Was there any way to salvage this mess? If only she'd look at him, maybe he could gauge his chances.

"Beau…"

"Yeah?"

She lifted a hand to the side of her face. "Can we go somewhere else to talk? Everybody's starin' at us."

Jodie was ashamed of him, didn't even want to be seen with him. What was the use of talking? "It's okay. You don't have to say it. I–I understand."

She caught his arm as he turned to leave. "Understand what?"

"I get it. You have a choice now. I'm not your only pass to freedom. You don't have to tell me you don't return my feelings; you don't have to try to let me down nicely. I get it." He'd told his father he'd meant what he'd said, and he had.

Looks like he'd made a laughingstock of himself again. Only this time the pain was worse—he wasn't sure he'd ever recover.

"But I do."

He looked at her in confusion. "You do? You do what?"

"I do return your feelin's." A small smile curved her mouth, raising his hopes. "I love you, Beau. I just don't understand how someone as amazin' as you could love me."

"You don't…" He couldn't believe what he was hearing. Apparently his speech earlier hadn't said enough. "Oh hang it all." Snatching her to him, he pressed his lips to hers and tried to get his point across another way, another oh-so-much-b—

"Ahem."

Beau jerked back at the familiar throat clearing. He didn't have to look to know his father stood right behind him.

Jodie stared up at him with dreamy eyes that made him want to pull her close again.

Father must've read his mind, because he cleared his throat again. Loudly. "*Ahem.* Do I take it that she has accepted your proposal?"

If the way she kissed him back said anything, she had, but he needed to hear more. "Jodie…what do you say? Will you… will you do me the honor of being my wife?"

Licking her lips, she leaned near and whispered, "Will you kiss me like that every day?"

With a barely restrained smile, he pressed a kiss to her ear and whispered back, "Gladly."

"I still don't understand how you could love me."

"I'll gladly show you how the rest of my life. You're one of a kind, Jodie Ross, and only a fool would miss that." He pulled back to see those sky-blue eyes he loved. "What do you say, sweetheart?"

"Yes…I'll marry you."

His wide grin matched hers as he leaned back in.

"Not until you introduce her to your mother."

Beau stopped a hairsbreadth from Jodie's lips. His father really knew how to ruin a moment. Jodie was right; they should've gone off somewhere else to talk.

Knowing his father would stick around until he got an answer, Beau stared at his bride-to-be. "Are you all right with that?"

"I haven't had a mama for years. I'd love that. Do you think she'll like me?"

"She'll love you." Beau dropped a kiss on her nose. "Father, do you think Mother would be opposed to traveling to Small Tree? I have a job to see to and a house to build—"

"A house?" Jodie's wide eyes searched his face.

"Yes, a house. My woman deserves a place to call her own."

Her smile grew, if that was even possible. "With a picket fence?"

"With a picket fence."

"And a puppy to play with in the yard?"

Beau suppressed a laugh. "I'm fine with a good guard dog."

"Oh Beau." She threw her arms around his neck. "I love you." She jerked away. "I'm gonna go tell Haskins I'm gonna work for him."

"Why?"

"The sooner we can buy all the materials, the sooner we can get the house built, and the sooner we can get married."

Beau's laugh broke free at her eagerness. "Whatever you

want, darlin'.""

"No daughter of mine is going to work if I have anything to say about it."

"Father!"

"Daughter?"

Beau took in the wonder on Jodie's face then looked at his father, only just realizing the significance of his word choice. Was he actually giving them his blessing? Earlier he'd questioned Beau's sanity.

Folding his arms, Father inclined his head. "You heard what I said." He relaxed his stance and gave Jodie a hint of a smile. "Young lady, you are a remarkable woman. It is quite an accomplishment, winning over a town and getting my son comfortable talking to the feminine sort, not to mention making him willing to stand up for you in front of a crowd *and* his father. She brings out the good in you, lad. Like a good wife should."

His chest swelling with pride, Beau slid an arm around Jodie's waist and tugged her a little closer.

"Consider the house a wedding present."

"But—"

"No *buts*, my boy."

Knowing it was senseless to argue, Beau nodded. "Thank you, sir."

"Very good. I will see you two at dinner." With that, his father strode toward town.

"I take it that was his way of invitin' us to dinner?"

"Yep."

Jodie cocked her head to the side. "I like him."

"The feeling seems to be mutual."

"But I'm still gonna work for Mr. Haskins."

"Or you could work with me…at least until the babies come."

"Beau!"

"What? You don't want to be my deputy?"

She pitched her voice to a whisper. "We can't talk about babies, can we?"

"Why not?" Surveying the area, he noted the schoolyard had emptied and pulled Jodie close. "We're alone, and we're engaged to be married. I think it's pretty natural to talk about babies. We'll need to know how many rooms to build on to that house."

Jodie leaned her head against his chest. "I can't believe all this is happenin'. Only this mornin' I was a prisoner wonderin' how many years I'd be stuck behind bars, my only family miles away. Now I'm a free woman, engaged to a wonderful man who wants to have a family with me. How did I get so blessed?"

"I've been wondering the same thing." Tilting up her chin, Beau touched his lips to hers, marveling at how what he'd thought had been a mistake—getting roped into a job he'd never asked for—had turned into one of the greatest blessings of his life.

Epilogue

Beau scooped up his sleeping granddaughter and placed her on the pallet next to her snoring brothers. Taking her place on the couch, he pulled his wife into his side and welcomed her head on his shoulder.

"I love that story." Jodie tucked her stocking feet onto the couch and leaned more fully into him. "Especially the ending."

"Do you still feel the same now as you did then?"

"Oh no."

"What?" He tilted to see her face.

She grinned. "I love you even more now than I did then."

"That's better."

Her quiet laugh warmed him, and he wrapped his other arm around her.

"You know, I still wonder the same thing I did then."

"What's that?"

He brushed a curl away from eyes still as blue and as beautiful as they were forty years ago. "How I got so blessed to have you."

"As do I, love." Lifting her face to his, Jodie met him with a kiss so sweet, so right, that it reinforced one thing he'd learned over the years—with God, there are no mistakes.

About the Author

Best-selling Christian Western author, born-n-raised Texan, and member of American Christian Fiction Writers, Crystal L. Barnes is the culprit behind the Marriage & Mayhem series and more. As an active member in the church since her youth, Crystal loves to minister however God leads her—be it through singing Southern Gospel, sharing her testimony of a marriage healed after twelve and half years of divorce, contributing to her church's worship and media teams, or helping other authors seeking to go the "indie" route. In 2021, her author services business took the name Better Way Publishing LLC. Find out more and connect with Crystal at www.crystal-barnes.com.

KEEP READING FOR A
SPECIAL EXCERPT FROM

SIGNED,
SEALED, &
DELIGHTED

Marriage & Mayhem, PREQUEL NOVELLA

BY CRYSTAL L BARNES

May 25th, 1877 – Wichita, Kansas

"Young man, this is normally when you say 'I do.'"

Joseph Matthews shifted his focus from Sarah Asher to the silver-haired preacher who stood grinning at him. Swallowing, Joe resisted the urge to tug at his collar. He'd sealed his fate with those two words weeks ago just before digging her father's grave, but today they threatened to crawl back down his throat and strangle him.

Allen Asher's bloody but relieved face flashed through Joe's mind. Shaking away the searing image, he wiped sweat from his forehead. That stampede had changed everything. That, and Allen's dying wish. His mentor knew Joe had no luck with women. Why had he made such an outlandish request? Why did marrying Allen's daughter have to be the only way to get the ranch he'd promised Joe, the ranch he'd put years of blood and sweat into?

"Son?" The old preacher shifted and placed a weathered hand on his Bible.

Twin lines formed between Sarah's dark brows.

"Uh, sorry." Joe rubbed at the tension building in his neck. "I do."

With a tilt of her head, Sarah eyed him, then turned her attention to the preacher who was posing the same question to her.

Joe let his gaze slide the length of his soon-to-be wife. Maybe marrying Sarah might not be so bad. After all, she was a mighty handsome woman. Even bathed in trail dust. And wearing a Stetson. A smile tugged at his lips. Did she realize she still wore her hat? Doubtful. What female in her right mind got married in a cowboy hat? Then again, who would confuse Sarah for most women? If her raven locks didn't set her apart, her mouth would the minute she opened it.

"I…" Deep green eyes wide with uncertainty sought his, then shifted back toward the preacher. "Excuse us a moment, Reverend?"

"Uh, of course."

Joe looked at the minister in stunned astonishment a split second before Sarah grabbed his arm and tugged him down the aisle of the small, stuffy church to within a foot of the exit.

"What's the matter?" The words hissed through his lips. "I thought this is what we'd agreed upon?"

Sarah peeked at the preacher, then answered in the same hushed volume. "There are a few things I need to make sure of first."

"You couldn't have mentioned that a day ago? Or maybe even an hour? The preacher's waiting."

"Do you want to keep your word to my father or not?"

Joe frowned. "You know I'm a man of my word. Now what's this about?"

"First—"

"You mean there's more than one?"

It was Sarah's turn to frown.

"I'm sorry for interrupting. Go on."

"First, you must agree that our sleeping arrangements won't change. When we get back to Texas, you'll stay in your cabin with your mother like always."

He rubbed his finger around the inside of his collar. That was not something he wanted to discuss with his future wife, especially in a church house. "'Til death did them part" was an awful long time to keep his distance from such a beautiful, spirited woman. Besides, how could he protect both her and his mother by living in a cabin fifty feet away?

"Your house is much bigger and has three rooms to boot. You, my mother, and I can all have our own. I'll agree to separate rooms, not separate houses."

She chewed on her lip a moment then gave a nod. "Fine. Separate rooms. Second, you let me do my work as I please without any interference."

"What work did ya have in mind?"

"That's my business."

"This wouldn't happen to have anything to do with you sneaking off to help that quack of a doctor, now would it?"

"He's not a quack." Realizing what she'd just revealed, she scowled at him.

"Sarah, you know your pa didn't approve of you working at that clinic, and I'm not going to have you endangering yourself. I promised Allen I'd take care of you, protect you. You can't ask me to break that word to him."

"And you can't ask me to stop helping people. I'll agree to keep your safety considerations in mind, but I won't be dictated to."

3

"Dictated to? What makes you think that's what I'm going to do? Besides, even the Bible says the husband is the head of the wife."

Pressing her lips together into a firm line, she took a step backward...toward the door. He swallowed hard. If he didn't think of something quick, she was going to make fulfilling his word to Allen a whole lot harder.

"Look, I'll do my best to reason with you and not dictate my wishes, unless something is truly dangerous to your wellbeing. Will that satisfy you?"

"What about the clinic?"

He swallowed a groan. "One day a week."

"Three."

"Two."

"Three."

"Mr. Matthews, are you two going to be much longer? My wife is expecting me home for supper."

"We'll be right with you, Parson." Joe shifted his focus back to Sarah. "Right?"

"Fine. Two, but there's one more thing."

Of course there was. Joe resisted the urge to roll his eyes. Why did women have to be so difficult? They'd given their word to her father. Couldn't they iron out all these details later? Nevertheless, he nodded for her to continue.

"I want my share of today's profits."

"*What?*" He lowered his voice when Sarah's eyes widened, and she stepped backward, her hand going to the doorknob. "I apologize. I didn't mean to shout. You're right. The money's as much yours as it is mine."

He reached into his pants pocket, pulled out the money, and counted out half of what he'd stuffed in there earlier after selling the beeves they'd brought to market. Of all the ridiculous things—paying a woman to marry him. But if that's what it took to keep his word...

Joe held out the money. "Here. Is there anything else? You want my horse too? My right arm?"

"I want it in writing."

"Writing?" Rubbing the tension knotting his neck, he turned. "Preacher, you got a piece of paper?"

Don't Miss the Marriage & Mayhem Series

Signed, Sealed, & Delighted
MARRIAGE & MAYHEM, PREQUEL NOVELLA

Her father's dying wish changes everything. Will signed promises seal Sarah and Joe's fate to a loveless marriage, or can Sarah move past her fears to find a love worth delighting in?

Win, Love, or Draw
MARRIAGE & MAYHEM #1

Sam McGarrett left with Catherine's heart and upended her home years ago… Now he's back. Can Sam win her trust? Will their love survive? Or will his final draw be his last?

Love, Stock, & Barrel
MARRIAGE & MAYHEM #2

Dinah's seeking answers but finds more than she bargains for when she gets caught in a shotgun wedding—with the rifle pointed at her.

Hook, Line, & Suitor
MARRIAGE & MAYHEM #3 (COMING SOON)

An heiress who's fishing for a husband. A widower who doesn't want to be caught. Could joining forces solve both their problems?

www.ingramcontent.com/pod-product-compliance
Lightning Source LLC
Chambersburg PA
CBHW020740130626
46554CB00006B/2076